Frances Anne Budge

The Barclays of Ury

And Other Sketches of the Early Friends

Frances Anne Budge

The Barclays of Ury
And Other Sketches of the Early Friends

ISBN/EAN: 9783337014544

Printed in Europe, USA, Canada, Australia, Japan

Cover: Foto ©Andreas Hilbeck / pixelio.de

More available books at **www.hansebooks.com**

THE

BARCLAYS OF URY

AND OTHER

SKETCHES OF THE EARLY FRIENDS.

BY

FRANCES ANNE BUDGE.

———

Reprinted from " FRIENDS' QUARTERLY EXAMINER," *with some additions,*

including

A SKETCH OF

SAMUEL WATSON AND ROGER HEBDEN,

———

"Faith is the victory over that which separated man from God."

GEORGE FOX

LONDON:

SAML. HARRIS & CO., 5, BISHOPSGATE WITHOUT, E.C.

——

1881.

' 'YE are not of the world,'—'I have chosen you out of the world,' were the words of our Saviour. The separation which our Lord intends for us is a separation from the world's spirit. Jesus Christ moved freely amongst His fellow-men; He sat down at the tables, and mixed in the company of all classes, yet was He most completely 'not of the world.' And we are called to follow the example of Christ, and bring our lives into harmony with His life and spirit. . . . Each one of us receives a light from God to show him the path in which he should tread, the way in which he is to walk, the work he is to do, and the manner of his self-denial. Let us all be willing to bring our own lives to the teaching of the Lord Jesus. . . . Then it is that we know how good the will of God is, and how acceptable to the humble waiting soul. We often hear about consecration and dedication of all to God. . . . 'Who then is willing to consecrate his service this day unto the Lord?' (1 Chron. xxix. 5.) I long that all our members may willingly bring all their substance, all their intellectual and physical powers, to the service of the Lord, saying :—'Here am I, Lord ; all that Thou hast made me, and with all that Thou has given me. I place myself in Thy blessed hands to do with me what Thou wilt.' The noblest form of enthusiasm is that where the soul and body and all their energies are completely given to the Lord Jesus."

STANLEY PUMPHREY.

I.

THE BARCLAYS OF URY.

"WITH the waves contending,
 See, the ships prevail,
Winning aid befriending
 From the adverse gale.
Thus the way contesting
 Souls must hold their course,
Thus a blessing wresting
 From each hostile force."

T. T. LYNCH.

"To Thee an ever-widening prayer
 Adoringly we bring,
That strength from weakness, joy from pain,
 And wealth from want may spring."

IBID.

THE BARCLAYS OF URY.

"As we firmly believe it was necessary that Christ should come, that by His death and suffering He might offer up Himself a sacrifice to God for our sins, who His own self bare our sins in His own body on the tree; so we firmly believe that the remission of sins which any partake of is only in and by virtue of that most satisfactory sacrifice, and no otherwise."—*Barclay's Apology*.

> " Up the streets of Aberdeen,
> By the Kirk and College Green,
>   Rode the Laird of Ury ;
> Close behind him, close beside,
> Foul of mouth and evil-eyed,
>   Pressed the mob in fury.
>
> .   .   .   .   .
>
> Yet with calm and stately mien
> Up the streets of Aberdeen
>   Came he slowly riding :
> And to all he saw and heard
> Answered not with bitter word,
>   Turning not for chiding."

Thus Whittier begins a spirited ballad describing an incident in the life of David Barclay. Once a distinguished officer in the army, now one of the persecuted Friends, he was insulted in his old age in the streets of the city where formerly public entertainments had been made in his honour. Presently a troop of cavalry passed by ;

> " Quoth the foremost, ' Ride him down !
> Push him ! Prick him ! Through the town
> Drive the Quaker coward !' "

But at that moment a scarred and sunburnt soldier,

who had shared many a danger with Colonel Barclay
in the past, recognised his old companion, and

> " Cried aloud ; ' God save us !
> Call ye *coward* him who stood
> Ankle deep in Lutzen's blood
>   With the brave Gustavus ?'
>
> ' Nay, I do not need thy sword,
> Comrade mine,' said Ury's lord :
>   ' Put it up, I pray thee :
> Passive to His holy will,
> Trust I in my MASTER still,
>   Even though He slay me.
>
> .   .   .   .   .
>
> Give me joy that in His name
> I can bear with patient frame
>   All these vain ones offer ;
> While for them He suffereth long,
> Shall I answer wrong with wrong,
>   Scoffing with the scoffer ?'"

David Barclay was the lineal representative of an
old and honourable family, and could trace back his
ancestry for upwards of 500 years to Theobald de
Berkeley, who lived in the days of David I., King
of Scotland. He was born in 1610, at Kirtounhill,
the birthplace and seat of his father, who was the last
laird of Mathers ; for, being careless in his expenditure,
and living much at Court, pecuniary embarrassments
compelled him to sell the estate of Mathers—which
had been in the possession of the family for 300
years—and also the old estate, which they had kept
for more than five centuries. He thus paid off his
debts and succeeded in giving his children a liberal
education.

As soon as his son David had left college he set out
for a tour in Germany, where he enlisted as a volunteer
in the army of Gustavus Adolphus, his courageous
conduct causing him to be quickly promoted to the

rank of captain, and then of major. Any further promotion was rendered impossible for the time, as, on the breaking out of the civil war, he was summoned home by his relations. He soon became colonel of a cavalry regiment in the Royalist army, having command of the shires of Ross, Sutherland, and Caithness. Some of his military exploits are still on record, but it was not his wont to allude to these in later life, when he could have said in the words of George Fox, "I cannot fight, for the spirit of strife is slain within me." He had enlisted in the army of the Lord of Hosts, who not only forbids revenge but commands the heartfelt forgiveness of all injury ; without granting His followers the option, which they are sometimes tempted to allow themselves, of saying, This wrong is too great, or that slight is too small for me to forgive "from the heart."

When Governor of Strathbogie, and at the age of thirty-eight, David Barclay married Katherine, daughter of Sir Robert Gordon, of Gordonstown, son of the Earl of Sutherland, and cousin to James I.

When, at the time of Charles the First's captivity in the Isle of Wight, the Scotch nation made a vigorous effort to rescue him, one army under the command of the Duke of Hamilton was sent into England; the protection of Scotland and of the person of the Prince of Wales—who was expected to land there—being meanwhile committed to three persons, of whom Colonel Barclay was one. The whole country, indeed, north of the Tay was confided to his care, at the head of his own regiment and 500 horse, a trust which he fulfilled with faithfulness and energy.*

When Cromwell came into power, Colonel Barclay

---

* "Colonel Barclay's locality was to be all benorth St. Johnston to Dings-bey-head, which was all Scotland benorth the water of Tay."—*Gilbert Gordon of Sallach.*

was dismissed from his post, and, finding himself unable to render further service to the Prince, he took up his abode at Gordonstown, where he lived for several years. After a time he purchased the estate of Ury, near Aberdeen, which became the seat of the family. He sat in several successive Parliaments, and was so popular that he had much influence in Scotland and particularly in his own neighbourhood. Letters from his constituents still exist, signed by the chief gentlemen of the shires he represented, containing thanks for the great services he had rendered his country. There is one from his cousin, the Earl Marischal, who, after returning a hearty acknowledgment for many favours, adds—"And that I may in some measure express it, . . . I have thought fit to signify that I shall be very willing to strengthen your conveyance by all that's in my power, as ye shall desire the same, with jovial heartiness. And I do entreat that when anything relating to me shall come before you, that ye will own the same for my interest and good. . . . My wife remembers her service to you, and we both to your lady and little Robin."

In 1663 David Barclay had the great sorrow of losing his excellent wife, whose dying request it was that their eldest boy, Robert, should be removed from Paris, where he was pursuing his studies in the Scotch Roman Catholic College, of which his uncle was the Rector. Here, as Croese says, he was " brought up in good literature, and after a manner that suited to his quality, and those noble youths that were his fellow-students." But his mother's heart was uneasy about his best welfare, though letters home had always told of the honours he was winning, and of the brilliant course that lay before him.

It was about this time that David Barclay—owing to some strange misapprehension, or fell design of depriving him of his estate and life—was committed a close prisoner to Edinburgh Castle. That this should be done by an order from Government after the Restoration caused great surprise, as Colonel Barclay had suffered much from his faithful adherence to the cause of the late King. When liberated, in consequence of the urgent interposition of his never-failing friend the Earl of Middleton, nothing whatever was laid to his charge, nor any reason assigned for his committal.

Colonel Barclay was now between fifty and sixty years of age, and for some time, with a keen sense of the instability of all earthly things, he had longed to devote the remainder of his days wholly to the service of the King of kings. But to which of the many religious bodies should he give his adherence ? The wide experience of the more active years of his life had given him the opportunity to observe their varied practices ; whilst the more recent and leisurely study of systems of divinity had made him familiar with their several doctrines. But each sect laid claim to be the only true Christians, and violently persecuted those who differed from them. In this perplexity he betook himself to the careful reading of the New Testament, yearning to know the religion of Christ in its first purity ; by which—so his eldest grandson records—" He came clearly to see the difference between what it was in itself, and the strange shape that several pretenders thereto had put it in ; that in itself it was love, peace, joy in the Holy Ghost ; that it taught to be humble, patient, self-denied, to endure all things and to suffer all things."

Strange stories of a people scoffingly called Quakers now reached his ears, which gave him the impression that if they were really such as even their enemies portrayed them, there was something so remarkable about them as to be well worthy of the most earnest investigation. He accordingly turned his whole attention to diligent inquiry relative to "this *way*," which was everywhere spoken against. And when in London, some months before his imprisonment in Edinburgh Castle, he clearly ascertained by conversation with the leaders of the Society of Friends there what they were setting forth as the truth of God ; and then (as a writer in the *Theological Review* remarks) "gripped fast by that truth with his whole soul, and never let it go." He noticed, moreover, that the Friends loved one another, and remembered that this was the test which Christ has given by which His disciples may be known ; and whilst he thought their principles coincided with the teaching of the New Testament, he observed that they practised what they taught. Of the inner working of his mind meanwhile we see nothing, but his subsequent life is a sufficient proof that earnestly seeking after truth he had " found Him of whom Moses, in the law, and the prophets, did write," and accepted Him as his Saviour and his Lord.

During his confinement in Edinburgh Castle he was much helped by earnest converse with an old comrade in arms, who shared his room, and who encouraged him to make an open avowal of his views, as he himself had done. This was Lord Swintoune, of Swintoune (an ancestor of Sir Walter Scott), who during his imprisonment seemingly cared more for spreading Christian truth than for defending his own life ; so that the governor of the castle, in the fear that he would press his " heretical " opinions on his fellow-prisoners, shut him up alone for several weeks.

This John, Lord Swintoune, nineteenth baron in descent of the old and once powerful family of Swintoune, had, in conjunction with Sir William Lockhart, of Lee, been entrusted by Cromwell with the chief management of Scotch affairs during the Commonwealth, when he sat in the Scotch Parliament, was one of the Lords of the Court of Sessions, and member of the Council of State. After the Restoration he was tried for his life. Bishop Burnet writes :—" He was then become a Quaker, and did, with a sort of eloquence that moved the whole house, lay out all his own errors, and the ill-spirit he was in when he did the things that were charged on him, with so tender a sense that he seemed as one indifferent what they should do with him ; and, without so much as moving for mercy, or even delay, he did so effectually prevail on them that they recommended him to the King as a fit subject for mercy." He was liberated after a long imprisonment.

Whilst the great change that had passed over the Laird of Ury did not cost him the friendship of the most generous and liberal of his acquaintance, it was yet the cause of insult and abuse from the low and malicious. In the north of Scotland, and chiefly at Aberdeen, the Friends were frequently mobbed by the dregs of the people, set on by the zealots of that day. Patient under oppression, unprovoked by unkindness, unmoved by scorn as the Friends usually were, it was said that none surpassed David Barclay in the calmness with which he bore these trials. On the occasion of some special indignity one of his relatives expressed sorrow that the laird should be treated thus in the city where he had once stood so high in public favour. But he replied that he now thought it a higher honour to be insulted for his religious principles than he had formerly considered it to be met by the magistrates some miles outside the city and escorted to a public banquet :—

> "Happier I, with loss of all,
> Hunted, outlawed, held in thrall,
>   With few friends to greet me ;
> Than when shrieve and squire were seen
> Riding out from Aberdeen,
>   With bared heads to meet me,

B

" When each goodwife o'er and o'er,
    Blessed me as I passed her door ;
  And the snooded daughter,
  Through the casement glancing down,
  Smiled on him who bore renown
    From red fields of slaughter."

David Barclay had counted the cost of his decision, and never doubted that he had chosen aright ; but he was desirous that his three young sons should be influenced only by their conscientious convictions. Two years before he joined himself in membership with the Friends he had, in compliance with his wife's dying request, gone to Paris to bring home his son Robert, who was then about the age of sixteen. So proficient was he in his studies that he had won the marked approbation of the masters of the colleges, and of his uncle, who had become so much attached to him as to be altogether unwilling to hear of parting with him. He offered to make Robert the heir of his considerable property, and also to purchase and immediately bestow upon him an estate larger than his paternal one on condition that he would remain with him. But Colonel Barclay preferred removing his son from Roman Catholic influence ; and, whatever the wishes of the latter might be, he answered his uncle's entreaties with the words : " He is my father, and must be obeyed."

After leaving France, Robert visited several relatives of both his father and mother, and thus had intercourse with Roman Catholics, Episcopalians, and Presbyterians. In early childhood he had been influenced by high Calvinists, and in his boyhood became for a time the proselyte of the Roman Catholics amongst whom his lot was cast. " In both these sects," he writes in his treatise on " Universal Love," " I had abundant occasion to receive impressions contrary to this principle of love ; seeing the straightness of several of their doctrines, as well as their practice of persecution, do abundantly declare how opposite they are to universal love." He forsook the Roman Catholic Church, and, for a time, attended various places of worship. During David Barclay's imprisonment in Edinburgh Castle the governor forbade any intercourse between the father and son for several months. But his father's example, and that of others who held similar views, impressed Robert Barclay's mind ; and he was especially helped by intercourse with Lord Swintoune and another Friend.

It would seem that it was in the meetings of Friends, which he now began to attend, that the Saviour revealed Himself to his seeking soul. In allusion to himself, he says, in "The Apology " :— " Who, not by strength of argument, or by a particular disquisition of each doctrine and convincement of my understanding thereby, came to receive and bear witness to the truth ; but by being secretly reached by this life. For when I came into the silent assemblies of God's people, I felt a secret power amongst them that touched my heart." It was when in his nineteenth year that Robert Barclay joined himself to Friends. He was soon afterwards sent by his father to reside on the estate of Ury, in company with their faithful agent, David Falconer, a Friend, who had frequently endured imprisonment for conscience' sake. A Friends' meeting for public worship was now opened at Ury, where David Barclay, ere long, settled with his family. This meeting, which was regularly held in a building close to the mansion, was continued for more than a hundred years.

We have no record of Robert Barclay's inner life during this marked crisis in it. Yet one cannot question that he had fully surrendered his heart to the Saviour who had redeemed him to God by His blood. For we are perhaps hardly able to estimate the sacri-

fices involved by the course he had taken ; sweetened
though they must have been by Him for whose sake
they were made.   To the refined and sensitive mind
outward persecution must have sometimes been a
lighter trial than was the surprise and dismay manifested by former acquaintance.   And great must
have been the disdainful astonishment awakened in
many minds, when first the gallant Colonel, and then
his highly-gifted intellectual son—Barclays " whose
coat armorial was overshadowed still by the shining
mitre of Aberbrothwick "—fell into " the scandalous
errours of Quaquarism "! for thus the tenets of
Friends were designated by the Presbytery of Brechin
in the diocese of David Barclay's brother-in-law,
Bishop Strachan.

Young Barclay now eagerly pursued his studies,
with the object of perfecting his knowledge of Greek
and Hebrew, and of thoroughly acquainting himself
with the history and writings of the early fathers of
the Church ; for the desire had sprung up in his heart
of composing a work on behalf of the sorely slandered
Society of Friends, which should be adapted by its
logical arguments to meet, on their own ground, those
schoolmen who attacked the views which had become
so dear to him.

Already he was a minister, and now, at the age of
twenty-two, his preliminary work—" Truth cleared
of Calumnies "—was published, the following short
extract from which is sufficient to show how full
was his belief in the completeness of Christ's salvation :—" What is the end of true religion but to lead
out of sin ?   Do the vitals of religion consist in *sinning* or *not sinning?*   If it consists in sinning, then
they who sin most are most religious.   But if it consists in not sinning, and keeping the commandments
of God without sin, then to plead for such a thing as
attainable hurteth not the vitals of religion.   What!

cannot the saints live better without sin than with it ? Yea, surely they can live well without that which is as a burden, and as death unto their life. They whose life is in sin cannot live but in sin ; but the saint's life is not in sin, but in righteousness."

When in his twenty-eighth year, Robert Barclay published in Latin the famous "Apology for the True Christian Divinity," some portions of which were evidently written for the express purpose of opposing the Calvinistic teaching of the Scotch " Shorter Catechism."

" It is his country's loss," remarks a writer in the *Theological Review*, " that his splendid *Apologia* should be left in the hands of a sect. Here, indeed, is a genuine outcome of the inner depth of the nation's worship; something characteristic and her own ; a gift to her religious life akin to her pro- foundest requirements ; and, if she did but know it, far worthier the thankful acceptance of her people than any reli- gious aid which she has ever welcomed from the other side of the Border. One great original theologian, and only one, has Scotland ever produced. . . . *No man ever gave Calvinism such mighty shakes as Barclay did. And he shook it from within.* He understood it. As the religion of his country he had entered into it, and made himself master of it. He had no half-measures of parleying with it. His controversy with Calvinism was on fundamental principles ; and while Calvin's axioms and postulates are of the waning past, Barclay's are of the widening future."

Besides the Latin and English editions the " Apology " has been printed in the French, German, Dutch and Danish languages. It is perfectly true that this work does not suit every kind of mind. Some of us may be quite unable to draw spiritual aid or refreshment from its logical pages. Yet, notwithstanding this, and although there are certain portions which, when taken separately, seem to be unguarded, whilst the young author's views on some points are perhaps extreme, we may well hope that it is a book that has not completed its work; and that "scepticism, dogmatism, and ritualism," as well as Calvinism, may yet find in its scholarly propositions, "an antidote for each." *

A clergyman of the Church of England, Mr. Norris, refers to Barclay as being "so great a man that I profess freely I had rather engage against a hundred Bellarmins, Hardings and Stapletons, than with one Barclay." Another remark about the "Apology," which seems worth quoting is from "Cato's Letters; or, Essays, Civil and Religious" (1720).—"It solves the numerous difficulties raised by other sects, and by turns thrown at one another, *and shows all parts of Scripture to be uniform and consistent.*"

It has been said that the primary reason for the publication of this work was to obtain, by a direct appeal to the sovereign, the justice so sorely needed by its author's misrepresented and suffering fellow-believers. And we can hardly doubt that this end was in measure attained, and that there was some ground for Voltaire's exaggerated statement that it "was surprising how this apology, written only by a private gentleman, should have such an effect as to procure a general release of the whole sect from the sufferings they then underwent."

Some idea of the extent of the persecution may be formed from the fact that about the year 1662 there were in England and Wales, at the very lowest computation, 4,200 Friends in confinement at one time. So closely were they crowded together in certain prisons that they had to take it in turn to stand up that there might be sufficient space for others to sit or lie down. Many died in consequence of the loathsome state of

---

* Are not Dr. Ralph Cudworth's words, written two centuries ago, applicable to the present age? "The sonnes of Adam are now as busie as ever himself was, about the Tree of Knowledge of good and evil, shaking the boughs of it and scrambling for the fruit; whilest I fear many are too unmindful of the Tree of Life."

their prison ; and others from the severe beatings they had received when their meetings were broken up.

The introduction to the " Apology " is addressed to Charles II. " There are tones in this preface," it has been said, " whose majesty of expostulation and calmness of admonition—with yet a thrilling earnestness which makes every syllable vibrate like a living thing —had never been equalled since Nathan took up his parable before David. The appeal was perfect, and it was successful."*

But whilst regarding Robert Barclay as an author we must not lose sight of him in private life. Early in 1670, the year in which his first work was published, and at the age of twenty-two, he married Christian Molleson, the daughter of " Bailie " Gilbert Molleson, a merchant and magistrate of Aberdeen. About twelve months earlier he wrote, apparently for the first time, to her. From this letter the following extracts are taken :—

" DEAR FRIEND,—. . . The love of thy converse, the desire of thy friendship, the sympathy of thy way, and meekness of thy spirit, have often, as thou mayst have observed, occasioned me to take frequent opportunity to have the benefit of thy company, in which I can truly say I have been refreshed, and the life in me touched with a sweet unity which flowed from the same in thee,—tender flames of pure love have been kindled in my bosom towards thee, and praises have sprung up in me to the God of our salvation for what He hath done for thee ! Many things in the natural will concur to strengthen and encourage my affection towards thee, and make thee acceptable unto me ; but that which is *before all and beyond all* is, that I can say, in the fear of the Lord, that I have received a charge from Him to love thee, and for that I know His love is much towards thee ; and His blessing and goodness is and shall be unto thee, so long as thou abidest in the true sense of it. . . . I am sure it will be our

---

* *Theological Review.*

great gain so to be kept that all of us may abide in the pure love of God. . . . In the present flowings thereof I have truly solicited thee. . . ."

This young lady, who was the same age as Robert Barclay, had become a Friend when in her sixteenth year, at the cost of hardship and suffering. Her father writes:—" I must confess shee hez beine the most Deserving chyld I have to me, as severall tymez that precious servant And Sanct of the Lord, hir Deceast mother Did witness."

Margaret Molleson, the mother thus lovingly alluded to, had lately died after the birth of her ninth child. In her youth she had hungered and thirsted after righteousness, and had been one of the first in Scotland to receive with joy the teaching of the Friends who visited that country bearing the glad tidings of a full salvation through Christ.*

A most loving and careful wife and mother, we yet learn that Margaret Molleson's " chief source of peace and joy, her chief desire, was to draw nearer and nearer to the true and living God, the beloved of her wrestling soul." Exceedingly often did she kneel before Him in private prayer, and, a faithful member of the little band of Friends at Aberdeen, she diligently attended their meetings. " I have lost a true Mary and a Martha," her husband said, " and none know how great my loss is ! " When she was thought to be dying, an eminent professor of religion, who was an old acquaintance, desired those who were in the room to pray for her. On hearing this she said :—" My advo-

---

* A *full* salvation, even deliverance from the law of sin by " the Spirit of life in Christ Jesus." Was not this the heartfelt and effectual message of the early Friends ? Where this is realised and taught, there, especially, God manifests His power, and souls are born anew. Now, as heretofore, " the great want of the *Church* is full salvation ; and the great want of the *world*, a Church full of faith and of the Holy Ghost."

cate is with the Father, and my peace is made. I am feeding at a table none of you perceiveth. . . . Now interruption is to cease, and my eternal joy is already begun."

Christian Barclay was worthy of such a parent; a good daughter, she was also a good wife and a good mother to her seven children. "No marriage," it has been said, "could have been more happy, more holy, or more blest." In patriarchal fashion Robert Barclay continued to reside at Ury after his marriage; Colonel Barclay spent some of the most peaceful years of his life amidst his young grandchildren. His eldest grandson records the impression of awe made on his childish mind by observing his stately and venerable grandfather's attitude in public prayer, when, Scotchman though he was, he always knelt, removing his hat with one hand and his black satin cap with the other.

About two years after his marriage Robert Barclay was imprisoned with Lord Swintoune and four other Friends, having been arrested at the conclusion of a meeting held at Montrose.

"We are in prison," they write, "quiet and in much love together. . . . The Lord is with us and on our side; . . . glory to His name, His arm, His power for ever! Who hath done it! and indeed it is well with us!" They addressed a letter to the Provost and Council of Montrose, expostulating with these magistrates for their conduct in confining them in the middle of winter in a cold and desolate prison; and also accusing them of desiring "to banish truth and a true people out of your coasts, or to vanquish them by tempting them to unfaithfulness, and to forsake the testimony which they are to bear among you—which they must bear and cannot forbear it. . . . As for us," they add, "we are not afraid of you, nor ashamed of our testimony, and you cannot vanquish us. . . . Our expectations—be it known to you—are neither from the hills nor from the mountains, but from God alone. Our case is committed to Him who judges righteously! We are, as regards our testimony and for its sake, well contented, well pleased, well satisfied to be here. Our bonds are not grievous to us: glory to the Lord for ever! who hath not been, who *is* not, wanting to us."

David Barclay's white hair did not save him from similar treatment. Some four years later he was taken, as well as many other Friends, out of a meeting at Aberdeen, and consigned to the Tolbooth. Robert Barclay was then absent on a ministerial journey in Holland and Germany, in the course of which he became acquainted with Elizabeth, the Princess Palatine of the Rhine, first cousin to Charles II., and a distant relative of Robert Barclay's mother. The Princess and her young friend, the Countess of Horne, gladly availed themselves of his religious teaching, and the Princess and himself soon afterwards began to correspond.

In her first letter, after a reference to Benjamin Furley, a Friend who had been his companion, she says :—

"Your memory is dear to me, so are your lives, and your exhortations very necessary. I confess myself still spiritually very poor and naked—all my happiness is that I do know that I am so—and whatsoever I have seemed or studied heretofore is but dust in comparison to the true knowledge of Christ. . . . Like your swift English hounds I often outrun my scent, being called back when it is too late. Let not this make you less earnest in your prayers for me; you see I need them. . . . I should admire God's providence if my brother [Prince Rupert] could be a means of releasing your father and the forty more prisoners in Scotland."

Prince Rupert's exertions were, it would seem, successful, for on Robert Barclay's return home he brought from London an order from the King for the release of his father. But, the Conventicle Act being still in force, the authorities of Aberdeen determined not to be baffled. Robert Barclay had not long resumed his happy home-life before they laid hands on him and confined him in the Tolbooth. On hearing of this, and with the fear that even his life might be in danger, the Princess Palatine wrote to Prince Rupert, who was then in London, begging him to do all that lay in his power to save Robert Barclay and his friends. "I care not," she says, "though his Majesty see my letter."

From his prison at Aberdeen Robert Barclay writes a letter to George Fox's step-daughters, Isabel, Sarah, Susannah and Rachel Fell, of Swarthmoor Hall. He encloses his first letter from the Princess for their perusal, knowing that he could confide it to their "discretion," and thanks them for a message of love in the postcript of a letter from their father. "Blessed be the Lord," he adds, "that has brought us to the knowledge of this kind of love and friendship which standeth in that which is more excellent than aught in the world, even in the Truth itself. And as we abide therein, it both may and can grow without finding an end. It was this precious Truth alone that brought us to an outward acquaintance as well as inward friendship."

We learn in what peace of mind the prisoners were kept, during their very painful captivity, by some remarks in a letter addressed to them by a Friend named Gavine Lawrie.

"Many a blessed night and day," he says, "have I felt when the body hath been in bonds; and I know the same life is with you. . . . Oh! how have I been filled with joy when I have heard how God's power hath broke forth amongst you in prison, and how the glory of the Lord hath filled your vessels! No news was so welcome to me. Yea, I have tasted of that joy with you. Dear friends, I could write much; but I know God's presence is *your all*, and is above *all* words."

God was with them, of a truth, and even here they could not keep silence, but, through gratings and loop-holes, spoke and preached to the passers-by. In

consequence of this, orders were given that five of the
Friends, including Robert Barclay and his father (who
soon had to follow him to prison) should be removed
to a place out of the town, down by the harbour, called
"The Chapel." Here they were shut up in a small,
cold, narrow place, which had a great door opening to
the ocean ; so dark was it that they could not see to eat
their food except by candlelight, or whilst the gaoler
held open the door when he brought their provisions.

Yet even in this vault they fared better than did the
companions left behind them ; for these were now
removed to the higher prison of the Tolbooth, in which
there was not room enough to lay their mattresses, and
where, whilst light and fresh air were excluded, the rain
found ready entrance. Their friends and some other
inhabitants of the town, fearing that their lives would
be sacrificed to this cruelty (for physicians admitted that
there was danger of this), now appealed to the magistrates on behalf of the sufferers. Bailie Barnet made
answer, that he would "pack them like salmon in a
barrel, and though they stood as close as the fingers on
his hands yet they should have no more room."

The imprisoned Friends now represented their case
in an address to the Council, and Robert Barclay having
been told that Archbishop Sharpe was one of the chief
instigators of this persecution, wrote a very plain letter
to him :—

"I presume," he says, "thou lookest upon it as thy chiefest
honour to be reputed a Christian bishop, deriving thy
authority from Christ and His Apostles. But *they* never
gave warrant for such doings ; being preachers and practisers
of patience and suffering, but never of persecution. . . . .
Thou mayst assure thyself that the utmost rigour that can be
used to us shall never be able to make us depart from that
living precious Truth that God, in His mercy, has revealed
to us ; nor fright us from the public profession of it ; yea,
though we should be pursued to death itself, which, by the
grace of God, we hope *cheerfully* to undergo for the same ;

and we doubt not that God would out of our ashes raise witnesses who should outlive all the violence and cruelty of man. And albeit, though thyself should be most inexorable and violent towards us, thou mayest assure thyself not to receive any evil from us therefore, who, by the grace of God, have learnt to suffer patiently."

Thus, whilst separated from his sweet wife and little children, and when in the power of his persecutors, did young Barclay write, for he had tasted of that perfect love which casts out fear. Nor need one pity him:

> " I could not choose a larger bliss
>   Than to be wholly Thine; and mine
> A will whose highest joy is this,
>   To ceaselessly unclasp in Thine.

> ' No liberty is half so sweet
>   As Thy constraining; let me be
> Engulphed within its vortex deep,
>   That Thou mayest live and reign in me." *

After a while the Commissioners decreed that, " considering the extraordinary trouble sustained by the magistrates and burgh of Aberdeen through the many Quaker conventicles held in the Tolbooth," some of the prisoners should be removed to the Tolbooth of Banff, whilst five of their number, of which David Barclay was one, should be set at liberty on condition that they would confine themselves to their country houses and parishes, and frequent no meetings. Strange to say they were allowed to accept their freedom, although they openly avowed that with regard to the restriction they must act as should seem right.

---

* " There is nothing," writes Dr. Ralph Cudworth, " in the whole world able to do us good or hurt, but God and our own will. . . . When we have cashiered this self-will of ours, which did but shackle and confine our souls, our wills shall then become truly free, being widened and enlarged to the extent of God's own will."

An order from the Council now led to much dispute between the magistrates of Aberdeen and the under-sheriff, who refused to convey the remaining prisoners to Banff, and urged the magistrates to find better accommodation for them, in accordance with the Council's order, which was of later date than the decree. So hot was this contention that each party entered formal protests at law with regard to the neglect of the other. During this quarrel, as both parties declined to accept of the disposal of the prisoners, Robert Barclay and five of his companions went before a notary and protested that they were "free men, and should pass away about their lawful occasions."

In the summer of this year, 1677, Robert Barclay, who was now nearly twenty-nine, accompanied William Penn during part of a religious visit to Holland and Germany. In conjunction with George Fox and some other Friends they had a very large meeting at Amsterdam, which began about eleven in the morning, and lasted for nearly five hours. Presbyterians, Baptists, Seekers, Socinians, and other sects came to it from far and near. "God was with His people," writes William Penn, "and His word of life and power, of wisdom and strength, covered them; yea . . . the mystery both of iniquity and godliness was opened and declared in the demonstration of the Eternal Spirit that day."

At Herwerden they had a warm reception from the Princess Elizabeth and the Countess of Horne, and frequent interviews with them and their friends. On these occasions the power of the Lord was much felt, and in two meetings held at the palace was remarkably manifested. Of the last of these William Penn writes :—"The word that never faileth them that wait for it, and abide in it, opened the way; . . . yea the quickening power and life of Jesus wrought and reached them; and virtue from Him in whom dwelleth the Godhead bodily went forth and blessedly distilled upon us as His own heavenly life."

As soon as the meeting was ended the Princess took William Penn's hand, and began to tell him of her consciousness of the presence and power of God in their midst; but her voice failed her, and, turning away towards the window she exclaimed, with the deepest and most uncontrollable emotion: "I cannot speak to you; my heart is full." William Penn was much moved, and spoke some soothing words to her. "We left them," he says, "in the love and peace of God; praying that they might be kept from the evil of the world."

The following day Robert Barclay started for Amsterdam, on his return to England. Whilst in the neighbourhood of London, on his homeward way, he replied to a letter from the Princess. After alluding to an interview with her cousin, the Duke of York (afterwards James II.), with regard to the persecuted Friends in Scotland, and to some information which she had given him, he says :—" My soul's desire for thee is that thou mayest more and more come out of all that cumbers, to feel this virtue of truth to operate and redeem thy soul out of all the difficulties that do or may attend thee." Then, having so often proved for himself the all-sufficiency of his Saviour's grace in every time of need, he continues :—" This, in the nature of it, it is powerful to do, albeit thy temptations were greater and more numerous than they are."

In 1679 Robert Barclay again visited Holland. It was also in this year that he obtained a charter from Charles II., under the Great Seal, constituting his lands at Ury a free barony, with civil and criminal jurisdiction to him and his heirs. The family retained this privilege until, in the reign of George II., the tenure of all such grants was put an end to in Scotland. Amongst Robert Barclay's numerous works are two treaties on the unlawfulness of all war.　One of these, written in Latin, was addressed to the ambassadors and deputies of the different sovereigns of Europe, who met at Nimeguen, in 1677, to " consult the peace of Christendom."　" He presented a copy to each of them, together with his principal work, ' The Apology for the True Christian Divinity.' "

His peace principles were practically tested on one occasion.　He was returning from the neighbourhood of London, where he had placed his son at a boarding-school, and the travelling party consisted of himself, his wife, her brother, and a Dutch gentleman. Whilst passing through Stonegate Hole, between Huntington and Stilton, they were attacked by highwaymen, one of whom pointed a pistol at Robert Barclay, who, taking hold of him by the arm, asked him, with perfect calmness, why he was so rude.　The robber trembled and let the pistol fall upon the ground.　Christian Barclay's brother was, however, robbed and roughly used, probably by others in the gang, and the poor Dutch merchant—it was thought accidentally—was shot in the thigh, the wound being so severe as to cause death in a few days.

In 1682, Robert Barclay was appointed Governor of East Jersey, in North America, by the Earls of Perth and Melford, and the other proprietors ; an appointment which was confirmed by the King.　The royal Commission states that " such are his known fidelity and capacity that he has the government during life ; but no other governor after him shall have it longer than for three years."　But Robert Barclay had no wish to leave his native land, and therefore only availed himself of the power with which he was invested by sending out as deputy a London merchant, Gavine Lawrie, to whom allusion has already been made as the writer of a letter to the imprisoned Friends at Aberdeen.

In the early part of 1685, Robert Barclay accompained his sister, Jean Barclay, to Edinburgh, and was present at her marriage with Sir Ewen Cameron, of Lochiel. He proceeded to London, and was for some time absent engaged in business on behalf of others. When at length he returned to Ury he was met by the sad tidings that his youngest brother, David, had died on his voyage to East Jersey, where he had intended to settle in company with his brother John. He was a young man of great promise, a Friend and a minister, and the stroke was keenly felt by his relatives, especially by his aged father, who soon followed him to his heavenly home.

David Barclay's death occurred in the year 1686. Neither violent fever nor great pain could cause him to utter one word or show one sign of impatience. "The Lord *is* nigh," he said, in reply to a remark of his son; "You are my witnesses in the presence of God that the Lord is nigh. The perfect discovery of ' the Dayspring from on high '—how great a blessing it hath been to me and my family ! " To his physician he said, "Bear a faithful and true witness. Yet it is the life of righteousness—*the life of righteousness* that we bear testimony to, and not to an empty profession." Repeatedly he said, " *The Truth is over all.*"

Robert Barclay only survived his father for about four years, which were spent chiefly in his own home, although he sometimes went to London to labour for the welfare of the Society of Friends. He endeavoured to turn his influence with James II. to good account on behalf of his brethren in religious profession who, although direct persecution had ceased, were still the victims of much oppression. His last journey to the metropolis was in 1688. As usual he did all that lay in his power to promote the interests of Friends, although the chief aim of his visit was to terminate a difference which existed between Sir Ewen Cameron and his powerful opponent, the Duke of Gordon. He was accompanied by his eldest son Robert, now a lad of sixteen, whose heart had been given to God from infancy ; the latter was now introduced to the Court at Windsor, and received much notice during his sojourn there. Probably his deportment stood out in strong contrast to that of many of King James's courtiers, for it is recorded of him, in reference to this time, that " his conversation was clean and void of offence, for he remembered his Creator in the days of his youth."

Robert Barclay left his happy home in 1690, to accompany James Dickenson, a minister from Cumberland, on a religious visit to some parts of the north of Scotland. Soon after his return he was seized with a violent fever : an intimate friend has recorded of him that he had never seen him in "any peevish angry temper," and—as might be expected—the all-sufficiency of his Saviour's grace did not fail to keep him in peace and resignation now. " God is good to all," he said ; " and though I am under a great weight of sickness and weakness yet my peace flows. This I know, that whatever exercises may be permitted to come upon me, they shall turn to God's glory and my salvation, and in this I rest." He died when in his forty-second year. His funeral was attended not only by sorrowing relatives and friends, but by several of the nobility and gentlemen of the neighbourhood ; and his son remarks that he was greatly lamented by all who knew him.

Some idea of George Fox's estimate of Christian Barclay's character may be formed from the strain in which he wrote to comfort her in her widowhood. "Thou and thy family may rejoice," he says, " that thou hadst such an offering to offer up unto the Lord as thy dear husband. . . . My dear friend do thy diligence in bringing up thy children in the fear of the Lord, and his new covenant of life. . . . Look at the Lord and serve Him with a joyful heart, mind, soul, and spirit, all the days thou livest upon earth."

Strength from that Saviour, whose she was and whom she served, was surely given her in that time of sore need. There was much yet to live for in the training of his young sons and daughters to follow in their father's footsteps, whilst her sympathies extended far beyond her home. "I observed," writes John Gratton, who spent some days at Ury, "that when her children were up in the morning she sat down with them before breakfast, and in a religious manner waited upon the Lord; which pious care and motherly instruction doubtless had its desired effect, for as they grew in years they also grew in the knowledge of the . blessed truth, and since that time some of them are become public preachers thereof."

Robert Barclay had seven children : Robert, Patience, Catherine, Christian, David, John and Jean, all of whom married; and Robert records fifty years after his father's death that they were all alive, and that his descendants at that time were between sixty and seventy in number.

It was some four years after the death of Robert Barclay that a minister, a Friend in humble life, named Peter Gardiner, left his home in Essex with the clear conviction that it was the Master's will that he should undertake a religious visit to Scotland. He had a family to care for, and was so poor that he could not provide himself with a horse for his long journey. His health was delicate also, and he was in some perplexity about the matter ; but the loving Lord, to whose will he resigned himself, granted him the assurance that neither strength nor means should fail him until his mission was accomplished. God's guidance was very remarkably manifested in giving him a perception of the spiritual state of those whom he visited, altogether unknown to him though they were. He suffered from no weariness, and said that he was now as much refreshed by a bit of bread and some water from a brook, as he was wont to be by a more sustaining meal. When, one day during his tour, a Friend insisted on seeing how much money he had, he could only produce two half-crowns, and it was hard work to get him to accept a little present. His labours in the neighbourhood of Aberdeen were attended by a remarkable outpouring of the Holy Spirit in the gift of Gospel ministry.

It was not likely that the children of Robert Barclay —albeit royal blood flowed in their veins—should close their hearts to the ministry of the stranger because his social standing was very unlike their own. On the contrary, it would seem that they at once welcomed him as an ambassador of Christ, and his visit to Ury was a time when blessing from the Lord flowed freely into their receptive young hearts. A good meeting was held one evening at Springhall, a house on the Ury estate, but Peter Gardiner spoke of his conviction that there were those present who were quenching the Spirit by keeping silence. After supper that night he had a sweet season with Robert, Patience, and little David Barclay, and some others, when Robert, who was now twenty-two, addressed a few earnest words to his young companions, which (writes one who was present) "reached and melted our hearts in a wonderful manner." He said it was he who had hindered the flow of spiritual life in the former meeting by being silent when Christ would have constrained him to speak; and he concluded in a brief but fervent prayer. In a meeting held with the young people on the following day, his sister Christian, who was about fourteen, engaged in prayer, to the refreshment of the souls of those present.*

---

* At the age of nineteen Christian Barclay became the wife of

Robert took some vocal part in the meeting held on the following Sabbath, when such heavenly power accompanied his words that some were touched, and others astonished. On the evening of that day a "blessed" meeting was held at Springhall, in which his sister Christian's voice was again heard, as well as that of Catherine Barclay, who was about sixteen, and their little brother David, a child of the age of twelve. After this Peter Gardiner was so firmly persuaded that the Barclays' young tutor was unduly keeping silence that he asked him " to clear himself." After he had spoken a few words, Peter Gardiner, with a thankful heart, concluded the meeting with prayer. A few days later, and after Peter Gardiner had left, the eldest sister, Patience Barclay, also felt that the Lord bade her open her lips for Him, testifying of His goodness, and in prayer.

In a letter to his friends at Aberdeen, where results similar to those at Ury had followed his ministry, Peter Gardiner told them of the blessing which had been also granted on his labours in the west of Scotland, where God was " pouring out His Spirit in a glorious manner." He admits that his inward exercise of soul had been " very great, yet is this matter of great joy that the work of my God is going on ;" words which recall Professor Upham's remark, " The cup of my happiness is full whatever may be my personal trials and sorrows, whenever and wherever my Heavenly Father is glorified in me."

In the early part of his journey Peter Gardiner had said that his Lord had bade him make speed with this visit, for he had but a short time to do it in. Soon after sending off his letter to Aberdeen, and whilst at

---

Alexander Jaffray, whose grandfather (of the same name) was so well-known in Scotland. She was a faithful labourer in the Gospel, and died when upwards of eighty ; her long life, " from early youth to her latest moments," being dedicated to her Lord.

Carlisle, he was taken ill of small-pox. "Ah, John," he said to a friend who asked him how he was, "I am sick in body, but the Lord reigns gloriously in Zion : *His power is over all His enemies.*" His words to a young visitor were : "I tell thee thou wouldst be heir to *two kingdoms*, but thou wilt never obtain them both." To his distant friends his last message was : "I have sweet peace with Him that is the Redeemer of Israel, and am now waiting for my pilot to conduct me to my long home."

Christian Barclay outlived her husband for thirty-three years, her bright and holy influence extending to her children's children, some eight or ten of whom usually enlivened the old home at Ury with their young voices and active tread. It was the aim of her life to minister to the spiritual and temporal need of others. The Friends of that neighbourhood wrote of their exceeding value of her ministry and friendship. It was her habit to assist and give advice to the sick, especially amongst the poor, some of whom came to her from a distance of more than forty miles. She died in her seventy-sixth year, in great peace and joy.

As we trace the lives and work of our forefathers in the faith, do we not ask ourselves, Wherein did their great strength lie ? But is the answer far to seek. Having recognised—not in mere theory, but in deep heartfelt experience—their absolute powerlessness to deliver themselves from the thraldom of the power of sin, they submissively placed themselves in the hands of the Lord who died for them, and found that His redemption was *full and complete*, and that at the bidding and by the power of Him who is the resurrection and the life, they could put off the old man and put on the new ; that the Comforter did come and abide with them for ever.*

---

* "If any man *wills* (Greek) to do His will, he shall know of the doctrine."

This crowning testimony was followed by others which, from their standpoint, formed part of a great whole. Christ Himself being their High Priest they needed no other. Baptised with the Holy Ghost, and having felt His sanctifying power, feeding continually on the Bread of Life, they needed not "The figures of the True; brought nigh by the blood of Christ, they lived in close communion with God, and to them any such mediums seemed only an obstruction between their souls and Him. They could not fight, for the spirit of strife was slain within them. Like the Apostles of old, they wrestled not against flesh and blood, but against principalities, against powers, against the rulers of the darkness of this world, against spiritual wickedness in high places ;" and " putting on the whole armour of God, . . . above all taking *the shield of faith*," whilst ever weak and unworthy in themselves, they were " more than conquerors through Him that loved them."

II.

JAMES PARNEL AND FRANCIS HOWGILL.

"I HAVE a CAPTAIN, and the heart
    Of every private man
Has drunk in valour from His eyes
    Since first the war began."

T. T. LYNCH.

"Then to side with Truth is noble
    When we share her wretched crust
Ere her cause bring fame and profit,
    And 'tis prosperous to be just;
Then it is the brave man chooses,
    While the coward stands aside,
Doubting in his abject spirit
    Till his Lord is crucified,
And the multitude make
    Virtue of the faith they had denied."

JAMES RUSSELL LOWELL.

JAMES PARNEL AND FRANCIS HOWGILL.

"I shall leave this as a query with all, both priests and people, . . . whether Christ is but a part Redeemer, or a perfect and full Redeemer."—JAMES PARNEL.

IN the year 1653 George Fox was for a time a close prisoner in the gaol at Carlisle. One musketeer was stationed at the entrance to his chamber, another at the foot of the stairs, and a third at the street door; and when the assizes were held it was rumoured through the town that he would be hanged. He had greatly offended the justices and magistrates, because when they examined him he had, as he says, "laid open the fruits of their priests' preaching, and showed them that though they were such great professors— for they were Independents and Presbyterians—they were without the possession of that which they professed."

The judge, justices and sheriff were, however, unexpectedly disappointed in their design of depriving him of life; and the only means in their power for wreaking vengeance on him was that of refusing him a lawful hearing, and thus leaving him in prison, where it was easy to secure his cruel treatment. Indeed, the gaoler had orders to put him into a most loathsome dungeon, with prisoners who were in such a horrible state that one woman was almost eaten to death by vermin. His companions were moss-troopers, thieves and murderers, whose carriage towards him was a strange contrast to that of his condemners. The power of God in which he dwelt so subdued them that they were, he writes, "all made very loving, and subject to me, and some of them were convinced of

the truth."*   The gaoler treated him with great
cruelty, but this could not hinder him from singing
the praises of the Lord.

It was during this imprisonment that George Fox
was visited by a lad, sixteen years of age, who was
actuated by a higher motive than that which animated
"the great ladies," who, at an earlier stage of his
captivity, had come "to see the man that was to die;"
but who would probably have left their curiosity un-
gratified rather than enter the dungeon which was
now his abode.   This youth was James Parnel, who
was born at Retford, in Nottinghamshire, in 1637.
When writing of his boyhood, he says that according
to his years he was "as perfect in sin as any in the
town," and remarks that many of the books he read
at school nourished "the wild, profane nature" which
then ruled in him.

He gained no advantage from his attendance at the
church at Retford; for he says that priest and people
alike were "walking in darkness and blindness, by
form, custom and tradition."   Yet the Holy Spirit so
strove with him in the depth of his soul, setting
life and death before him, that he would secretly
resolve never again to be guilty of some sinful folly.
But these determinations, made in his own strength,
were soon swept away by the tide of temptation.
"There was," he writes, "as little hopes of my con-
version as any in the town, and yet, though it is a
place of many people, I was the first in all that town
which the Lord was pleased to make known His

---

* In one of his epistles George Fox writes.—" In the power of
the everlasting God—which comprehends the power of darkness,
and all temptation and that which comes out of it—in this power
of God dwell; . . . and into that the tempter cannot come, for the
power and truth he is out of, . . . and let your faith be in the power
and over the weakness and temptations, and *look not at them; but,
in the light and power of God, look at the Lord's strength, which
will be made perfect in your weakest state.*"

power in, and turn my heart towards Him, truly to seek Him, so that I became a wonder to the world." The change was a complete one; henceforth he was to glory only in the cross of Christ, whereby the world was crucified to him, and he unto the world.*

"If any man be in Christ he is a new creature;" mere worldly customs, fashions, and modes of worship were now altogether alien to him; and the world that hated the Saviour whom he followed hated him also. There were some who said that his murder would be a service to God; worst of all his own family became his bitterest enemies. He was not then fifteen years of age, and, being small of stature, must have looked a mere child. But how often "God hath chosen the weak things of the world to confound the things which are mighty; . . . that no flesh should glory in His presence":—

"Once for the least of children of Manasses
God had a mission and a deed to do;
Wherefore the welcome that all speech surpasses
Called him and hailed him greater than he knew."

"He that hath called me by His power," James Parnel writes, "kept me, and gave me strength to bear His cross and despise the shame; so that *neither foul words nor fair words could cause me to deny what God by His grace had wrought in my heart.* But by His power He carried me above the raging waves of the tempestuous sea."

The clergy opposed him and said he was deluded, for his changed life was a protest against their own; yet they had let him alone in the days of his sinful-

---

* "It is life; it is the only life that may satisfy all my being, to be nothing, and to have Christ. Oh, trust Jesus to bring you into full fellowship with His dying. Trust Him; don't look to your nature, to your feelings. Behind the valley of death, there is abundance of life.—*Stockmayer.*

ness. He now longed to find some with whom he
might have Christian fellowship, and discovered. that
there were those only a few miles off " whom the Lord,"
he said, " was gathering out of the dark world to sit
down together and wait upon His name." It is true
that in uniting with them he had to share in the
persecution to which they were the victims, but to
this he gave little heed, being lifted above the suffering
by the knowledge that it was borne for the sake of
the Lord who had died for him.

After a while he heard of some Friends in the North
of England, and was constrained to seek for intercourse with them, feeling united to them in spirit
although he had never seen their faces. At Carlisle,
as we have already seen, he visited George Fox in his
dungeon. The latter, who was then about thirty-one,
alludes to James Parnel, in his Journal, as a little lad
of about sixteen years of age ; and adds, " The Lord
quickly made him a powerful minister of the word of
life, and many were turned to Christ by him, though
he lived not long."

It is easy to imagine something of the sweet spiritual
intercourse between the two in that dreary dungeon,
with its motley inmates. After all it was a fitting
place to be the scene of James Parnel's deeper instruction in the things of God ; and even if there were a
momentary sinking of his young heart as he saw in
George Fox's treatment the consequences of the stead-
fast upholding of a pure religion, we may well believe
that he also tasted something of that perfect love
which casts out fear, and which would make it easy to
suffer great things for the sake of Him whose will was
becoming the centre round which his life revolved.
After his return from the North he pursued his outward calling ; " the Lord," he writes, " all this time
still more and more perfecting and increasing His
work in my heart, and by His pure power bringing
forth His truth in me, and making known His will

unto me, until by His power He opened my mouth to declare His truth in the world."

When in his eighteenth year James Parnel, constrained by the love of Christ, visited a place fifteen miles distant, where the Lord was reviving His work. Soon the town of Cambridge was so brought before his mind that he felt he must go there to see what the Lord had for him to do, although he knew not one foot of the way nor what reception he should meet with; except indeed that he had heard that two of his friends had been whipped by order of the mayor, because they had preached there when passing through. Yet he says, " He that called me forth went along with me and did direct me." When he arrived there he found some who were ready to welcome his visit; amongst others a Friend who had already suffered imprisonment for teaching truths similar to those which had become so dear to him, and which the Lord was even now calling him to make known to others.

Before a fortnight had elapsed the mayor committed James Parnel to prison for the publication of two papers on "The corruptions of the magistrates and priests." This imprisoment was shared by Richard Hubberthorne, who, on September 4th, 1654, says, in a letter to Francis Howgill :—" James Parnel and I are in the dungeon as yet, where we were put the 28th of last month; but we feel the mighty power of God, and are in joy and peace in the Lord ; to Him be praise eternal !" James Parnel might have retained his liberty had he consented to give bond for his " good behaviour." But this he could not do, knowing the construction that might be placed on these words. " I am redeemed," he said, " out of the generation [which is guilty] of misdemeanours; and am bound to good behaviour by a stronger bond than man can make." He was moved from prison to dungeon, or from dungeon to prison, during two sessions, for his adversaries were unable to charge him with any breach of the law.

At the second session a jury was summoned with the intention that the papers which had been published should be stigmatised as " scandalous and seditious." But the verdict brought in by the jury was that they " found nothing but that the papers were his," a fact which he had himself acknowledged in open court. Yet he was detained a prisoner for three days longer, and then sent out of the town with " a pass, under the name of a rogue," and accompanied by an escort armed with clubs and staves. He lodged at a house three miles out of the town, whither he was followed the next day by a justice of the peace, who, being well aware of his innocence, asserted that the pass was false, and, taking possession of it, set him at liberty.

Not long afterwards he again visited Cambridge and its neighbourhood, " preaching and declaring the truth freely,—and many [he adds] I found that received the truth gladly, but more enemies, yet, nevertheless, Truth spread and conquered." He thought it right to engage occasionally in public disputations. It would seem to us that James Parnel's language was too condemnatory in some of these debates as well as in his controversial writings, although no doubt the current customs of that day afford some explanation of this style of expression. The tone of his life may well lead us to believe that, in common with other of his brethren in the faith, he aimed only at waging war with the *evil nature* in those who violently opposed the truths he advocated. His private character was marked by meekness, gentleness, and patience : and a beautiful instance of the manner in which he received personal injury is thus quaintly recorded by his friend Stephen Crisp :— " Some undertook to club out the priests' and professors' arguments by beating this dear lamb with fists and staves; who took all patiently, as particularly one who struck him with a great staff, and said, 'Take that for Jesus Christ's sake;' to which he returned the answer, ' Friend, I *do* receive it for Jesus Christ's sake ! ' "

It was arranged that one of these discussions should take place at Cambridge in April, 1655, when Francis Howgill and Edward Burrough, who were just then in the neighbourhood, joined James Parnel. The Baptists had fixed that the meeting should take place in a chapel, but when they came to it they found themselves shut out. The town was in an uproar, in which the young collegians took a prominent part. After a while a message was sent to James Parnel to inform him that the Baptists were in a public hall in the Castle-yard, and had sent for him. Here he found a Baptist, named Doughty, and one Rix, a brewer, who was an Independent; "Two great enemies," James Parnel says, " one against another, in opposition against each sect,—yet these two were joined together as friends against me." He now had an opportunity for addressing those who had assembled, but only one question was asked by his opponents, who were dissatisfied with his reply, and pronounced it to be no answer. Indeed, Doughty stood up hat in hand, and, beckoning to the young collegians, said, " Judge ye, gentlemen of divinity." A drunken clergyman made common cause with the rabble by siding with the Baptist party ; but some of the students and " many simple hearts," as James Parnel says, were satisfied with his answer. Doughty requested that James Parnel should not be allowed to remain in the hall after his own departure, lest he should seduce the people ; and as James Parnel quitted the Castle-yard he was violently attacked by a group of the wild young collegians, whilst his opponents passed quietly away; " So it appears," he says, " the world loves its own."

Howgill and Burrough apparently did not take any-part in this disputation.   A month later James Parnel addresses a letter to them from Cambridge, in which he tells them of his experience in that neighbourhood ; relating how at Ely he was "mightily preserved" by God, and was enabled to speak with much power in a large meeting, so that many hearts were reached, although the townspeople, as a whole, seemed to be quite hardened against true religion.   At Littleport he had left behind him a meeting of some sixty persons ; at Soham he spoke "in demonstration of the Spirit and of power" at the conclusion of a service in a church, where he was so thronged by the rough people that he pressed through their midst into the churchyard, and they stood around him "even like lambs," as he continued to address them.   The next morning he was committed to prison, and confined in a low gaol amongst thieves ; but on the following day a justice of the peace named Blackley (probably the justice who had befriended him before) sent a warrant and set him free.   "But," adds James Parnel, "I was made very willing to remain if it had been the Lord's will ; but in His large wisdom He ordered it according to His good will and pleasure, for I did not motion it to Blackley, but he did it of his own accord."   In allusion to his belief that some were plotting together to get him into prison again, he says :—"But according to the good will of God be it ; as it stands to His glory I am content whether in bonds or out of bonds."

He probably imagined that this long letter would be read by many of his friends, for he begins thus : "Dear friends and brethren,—In the eternal, unchangeable love and life of the new Covenant am I with you, and there do salute you, where we are one (in our measures) though ten thousand ; all children of one Father, brethren and sisters of one family."

About a year earlier Francis Howgill and Edward Burrough, the former aged thirty-six, the latter eighteen, had come to London from their homes in the Yorkshire dales, and are said to have been the first Friends who publicly preached in London. Endued with power from on high, going forth at the bidding of Him to whom they wholly surrendered themselves, we cannot be surprised at the results which followed their labours. "Hundreds are convinced"—we find them writing—"and thousands wait to see the issue."

James Parnel—after spending some six months in Cambridgeshire and Huntingdonshire, where, he says, "Truth spread and conquered over its enemies"—passed on into Essex, having heard of "a people" there who were earnestly seeking the Lord. Here he found the fields white unto harvest ; many who were weary with the weight of unforgiven sin, and many also who were no less weary with their vain efforts to free themselves from it. Others there were indeed who, we are told, had "built their tower of profession so high they conceited it did touch heaven itself." It was not these, but the poor and needy souls ready to despair of deliverance, who eagerly listened to the truths proclaimed by the preacher, as he published the glorious Gospel of life and salvation. He visited Felsted, Stebbing, Witham, Coxal, Halstead, and several other places, where his message was effectual in turning many from the power of Satan unto God. He spent some time in Essex, where he established several good meetings, and confirmed the faith of those that had believed. In the middle of the summer he came to Colchester, and on the day after his arrival preached to thousands of people.

Amongst his hearers on that Sabbath day was a young man, of twenty-seven, named Stephen Crisp, who had greatly desired that one of the Quakers, of whom he had heard so much, might come and preach in his native town. He had studied the sacred Scriptures and various old philosophical works, but his soul yearned for a closer and more personal

knowledge of Christ than he yet possessed. At one
time he hoped to obtain help by being baptised, but
soon found that no outward washing has power to
cleanse the soul. He went to various churches and
chapels, but not a word could he hear with respect to
winning the victory over sin.

More than thirty years later, in a powerful sermon
taken down by one of his hearers, Stephen Crisp says:
" What comfort can a serious Christian take in a faith
that falls short of righteousness and redemption?
Would it not make a man or woman's heart ache to
think—I am a believer, but yet I have no faith that
reacheth to sanctification and holy living and redemption from sin? . . . Who was ever so mad as to
suffer for such a faith as will leave a man under the
power of Satan and his own lusts. No wonder that
such have a faith that is not worth contending for
nor suffering for.

James Parnel's ministry was an effectual message
to Stephen Crisp, which can be easily imagined if he
preached as he wrote of Christ; as of " One who is
now come to redeem unto Himself a pure people, and
to wash them and cleanse them from their sins by His
own blood, and to wash away all filthiness both of
flesh and spirit." " Praised be the Lord," he again
writes, " We do witness a freedom from sin by Jesus
Christ, who is the Lamb of God, who came to take
away the sin of the world, and to redeem His people
from their sins."

When describing James Parnel's remarkable labours
on that day, Stephen Crisp says, "The wisdom, power
and patience of Christ appeared very gloriously, to the
convincing of myself and many more who were witnesses of that day's work." Yet at first Stephen Crisp,
observing his youth, sought to argue with him, but
soon discovered that James Parnel's belief was built
upon too sure a foundation to be shaken. After
alluding to his own mental suffering before he yielded

up self-will, self-confidence, and self-righteousness, Stephen Crisp writes, " But, O ! how glad was my soul when I had found the way to slay my soul's enemies. O ! the secret joy that was in the midst of all my conflicts and combats. Then the reproach of the Gospel became joyous to me ; though in those days it was very cruel to flesh and blood !

For ten days James Parnel laboured in Colchester in preaching, prayer, and exhortation, and many heard and believed ; whilst others manifested their opposition by insults which were not intolerable because they were met by perfect patience. From Colchester he went to Great Coggeshall, where a day was appointed for a public meeting, fasting and prayer, " against the errors of the people called Quakers." James Parnel knew that they hoped · to ensnare and imprison him ; but he was pressed in spirit to go there, and was willing for his Saviour's sake, "not only to be bound, but also to suffer for the pure eternal truth ! " He was soon committed to the common gaol, Colchester ; and when the time for the Chelmsford Assizes arrived, he was led through the country as a gazing-stock," closely chained with felons and murderers by night and day. But Christ's grace was sufficient for him. God was glorified, and he was content ; for he says, " But Truth was preached in all this, and prevailed on the hearts of the people, so that I could rejoice in all."

At the Assizes, James Parnel, as if the chief offender, was first led into the Court. Although the chain was removed before he was brought before the bar, he had irons upon one hand ; but as some of the people exclaimed at this severe treatment they were taken off on the following day before he left the prison. A long indictment, full of falsehoods, was read ; he pleaded " not guilty," but two justices of the peace and an Independent minister swore falsely against him. Before the jury (who had a drunkard for their foreman) left the Court, the judge endeavoured, when summing up

the case, to incense them against the prisoner, telling
them that if they did not find him guilty the sin
would be upon their heads.   But on their return they
said they could charge him with nothing but the
writing of a paper in reply to his mittimus, for the
imputations contained in the indictment were false.
During the trial the judge had allowed some of James
Parnel's accusers to stand on the bench and whisper
in his ear, and now he contrived to draw some remark
from the foreman of the jury (with which the other
members of it did not agree) and on its strength he
arrogated a legal right to fine James Parnel and re-
commit him to prison.   Yet the prisoners arraigned on
the suspicion of murder and felony, were, it would seem,
acquitted.   James Parnel observed that the manifest
injustice with which he was treated impressed the
people who were present, and, believing as he did that
even then " the Truth was owned by many hearts,"
his sufferings were made joyous to him.   " They
brought me back to prison again," he writes, " where
I still remain in the peace and freedom of my spirit,
which none can take away though in the hands of
mine enemies." His conscientious refusal to pay the
unjust fines imposed on him, was apparently the excuse
for this renewed imprisonment.   In a letter to the
judge he said, " If I should pay one penny for the
liberty of body in this cause, it would be as much as
if I paid the whole fine which thou hast unjustly laid
upon me ; for by so doing I should own myself a
transgressor where I am not guilty.   And also, a
bought liberty would be a bondage to my spirit ; but
the liberty which I have, even under thy bonds, is
bondage to thee.   And this liberty thou canst not rob
me of by all that thou canst do, for it is *the free gift
of God.*"
 The judge had especially charged the gaoler not to
allow James Parnel to receive visits from " any giddy-
headed people," as he chose to style the prisoner's

friends. But James Parnel's interest was deep in those to whom he had been the instrument of blessing, and many were the epistles that he now wrote to particular persons, and to the Meetings in general. In one of these, addressed to the Friends in Essex, we find the following passage :—

" Out of yourselves you must come. . . . If you hearken unto self then you stumble in the way, and many hardships and impossibilities do appear before you; and doubts and fears and questionings and murmurings, repinings and unbelief rise in you, and many temptations betake you. . . . Sometimes after the delights and flesh-pots of Egypt; sometimes that God hath utterly forsaken you; sometimes questioning the very truth of God. And here is the wavering and unstable mind, all which ariseth out of darkness where self stands—*all which comes by hearkening unto self.* Therefore, unto the Light (John i. 9)—the Messenger of God—keep your minds, which brings the message of peace and glad tidings of salvation; to which keep close. . . . This is the Word in you (John i. 14) from whence comes faith which makes all things easy and possible; . . . which judgeth down all murmurings, doubtings and repinings, all carelessness, lightness and earthliness."

This extract may remind us of Whittier's lines :—

" We turn us from the light, and find
 Our spectral shapes before us thrown,
As they who leave the sun behind
 Walk in the shadows of themselves alone.

 . . . .

" A voice grows with the growing years ;
 Earth, hushing down her bitter cry,
Looks upwards from her graves, and hears,
 ' *The Resurrection and the Life am I.*'

 . . . .

" All souls that struggle and aspire,
 All hearts of prayer by Thee are lit ;
And, dim or clear, Thy tongues of fire
 On dusky tribes and twilight centuries sit.

 . . . .

> " O Beauty, old, yet ever new !
>   Eternal Voice and Inward Word,
>   The Logos of the Greek and Jew,
>   The old sphere-music which the Samian heard !

> " Truth which the sage and prophet saw,
>   Long sought without, but found within,
>   The Law of Love, beyond all law,
>   The Life o'erflooding mortal death and sin !"*

The visitors who were admitted to the prison were such as came for the sake of scoffing at him and striking him. The gaoler's wife set her man to beat him, whilst swearing that she would have his blood. To which James Parnel would reply, " Woman, I will not have thine !" At one time his food would be kept from him ; at another his fellow-prisoners would be bidden to steal it. He was not allowed the comfort of a trundle bed which some of his friends provided, but had to lie on a stone floor which was frequently wet with rain. In a letter to William Dewsbury (then a prisoner in Northampton gaol), whom he addresses as his " Dear and precious brother in the eternal, unchangeable truth of God," he says, " they have laboured to make my bonds grievous, but my strength the Philistines know not." He might have said, in the words of a modern poet :—

> " I am persuaded that no thing shall sunder
>   Us from the love that saveth us from sin ;
>   Lift it or loose hereover or hereunder,
>   Pluck it hereout, or strangle it herein."

After a while he was not allowed the use of a room. In the walls of the castle, which are of extreme thickness, are two rows of vaulted holes, and in one of these, twelve feet above the ground, he was now con-

---

* " And I saw there was an ocean of darkness and death : but an infinite ocean of light and love flowed over the ocean of darkness. And in that I saw the infinite love of God."—*George Fox's Journal.*

fined.   He was furnished with a ladder, but as it was only six feet in length, his sole resource for obtaining any food was by descending and ascending the remaining six feet by the aid of a rope.   His friends would have given him a basket and cord for drawing up his rations had they not been forbidden to do so.   In this miserable abode his limbs became benumbed, and one day, whilst attempting to return to it, he missed his footing and fell to the ground.   So grievously was he injured that he was taken up as dead.

He was next placed in one of the lower holes in the wall, which was called the Oven; it was extremely small, and had no opening for the admission of light and air.   When he had regained a little strength he once asked leave to go out into the air, being exceedingly exhausted for want of it; but this request was refused.   A Friend, named Thomas Shortland, offered to take his place—" to lie body for body "—that James Parnel might come to his house until he had recovered ; but this proposal was declined by the authorities, as was also a bond of £40 offered by two other Friends. In the midst of all this suffering he must have been cheered by the knowledge of the abundant increase which God was giving to his bountiful sowing of the seed of the kingdom.

When some ten or eleven months had elapsed his constitution could no longer endure the terrible strain upon it.   His friends, Thomas Shortland and Ann Langley, were now allowed to visit him.   " Here I die innocently," he said to them.   " Now I must go. Thomas, I have seen great things.   Do not hold me, but let me go."   Then, in his longing to depart, he added, " Will you hold me ? "   Ann Langley answered, " Dear heart, we will not hold thee."   Then, stretching himself out, he said, "Now I go," and fell into a sweet sleep, drawing his last breath in about an hour. He had often said, "One hour's sleep would cure me of all."   He died at the age of nineteen.

Let us now turn our attention to a few details concerning Francis Howgill. George Fox's visit to Yorkshire had been the means of wonderful blessing to him and his young friend Edward Burrough, both of whom had before that time been deeply exercised with regard to the things of God. Francis Howgill writes :—

"I fasted, prayed and walked mournfully in sorrow. . . . I ran to this man and the other and they applied promises to me, but the witness of Christ showed me that the root of iniquity stood, and that the body of sin was whole. . . . Then I told them there was guilt in me. And they said sin was taken away by Christ, but the guilt should still remain while I lived. . . . So I said in myself this was a miserable salvation that the guilt and condemnation of sin should still stand in me. . . . Yet often I was made to do many righteous things by the immediate power of God and then peace and joy sprang up in me, and promises were spoken that He would teach me Himself and be my God ; I often obeyed contrary to my will and denied my will."

He had united himself to one sect after another without finding what he so earnestly sought for ; yet he frequently preached, feeding others—as he afterwards saw—with words alone. At the time of George Fox's visit to the Dales, Francis Howgill, who possessed some literary acquirements, filled a rather prominent position among the religious professors of that neighbourhood. One day, when attending a fair at Sedburgh for the hiring of servants, he met with George Fox, and heard him preach in the churchyard, exhorting his hearers " to come out from the temple made with hands, and wait to receive the Spirit of the Lord that they might know themselves to be the Temples of God." Francis Howgill was deeply impressed by his ministry, and when a military officer interrupted the preacher by some remark, exclaimed, " This man speaks with authority, and not as the scribes." Many that day received the glad tidings with joy.

On the next Sabbath morning Howgill preached at
Firbank Chapel, in Westmoreland, to a crowded congregation. Before noon George Fox arrived at this
place, and, whilst others went to get dinner in the
interval between the two services, having quenched
his thirst at a stream, he sat down on a rock near the
chapel. Soon the people gathered around him until it
was supposed that they numbered above one thousand ;
and for about three hours George Fox "declared
God's everlasting truth and word of life freely and
largely." "I believed the eternal word of truth,"
Francis Howgill writes, "and the light of God in my
conscience sealed to it." He now saw that hitherto
he had known far more of the form of godliness than
of its living power. "All was overturned," he says; "I
suffered the loss of all. Then something in me cried,
'Just and true is His judgment!' . . . But as I bore
the indignation of the Lord something in me rejoiced;
the serpent's head began to be bruised. . . . Then I saw
the cross of Christ and stood by it, and the enmity
was slain by it. . . . And the holy law of God was
revealed unto me, and was written in my heart. . . .
And so it pleased the Father to reveal His Son in me
through death, and so I came to witness cleansing by
His blood, . . . and have rest and peace in doing
the will of God, and am entered into the true rest,
and lie down in the fold with the lambs of God,
where the sons rejoice together. Glory unto Him for
ever !"

The remaining sixteen years of Francis Howgill's
eventful life were devoted fully, freely, and effectually,
to the service of his Redeemer. And it was no half-
gospel that he preached. In one of his numerous
works he bids the honest-hearted who have found no
rest to their souls not to seek to know God in their
own fallen wisdom, since the well is too deep for them
thus to get one drop of living water. He tells them
to arise, to dwell no longer amongst the graves and

tombs. Christ was risen. He was not there. His proclamation was that every one who thirsteth may come without money and without price; " *Without,*" so Francis Howgill adds, " *anything of yours or self; nay self must be denied if you will receive of Him that He may be all and you nothing, for He gives freely,* and His gift is perfect and pure, without spot, stain or mixture."*

Francis Howgill goes on to say, that as they come to be redeemed from the bondage of sin, there will be a " delight in doing the will of the Father, because they are redeemed from sin and its law to righteousness and its law."

In an "Epistle to Friends in London," he remarks :—

" Destruction is of self, and barrenness is of self, and deadness and disobedience are of self. But as you believe in Him who is near, and in His grace, and the word of His grace, self is judged and bruised under, and you will feel Him who is the First and Last to enlarge your borders and make your mountain strong, and your heritage goodly, and your ground fair and pleasant, when the pleasant fruit of righteousness is brought forth."

And, again :—

" That is not a true faith which is imperfect, and which lays hold upon an imperfect righteousness; that is such a faith as never was professed by any of the saints. For they had received faith, the gift of God. And as they stood in it, though it was but a grain of mustard, they said to this mountain, ' Be removed,' and it was so. And that which was in them revealed by the Son, led them that did believe in it to lay hold upon Christ's righteousness. . . . *And this was the righteousness of faith, and that which was wrought by Christ in the saints as they believed in Him, and in the measure of*

---

* " From every point of view and under all forms, the Apostle repeats the great truth (with which he was himself penetrated, and which forms the central point of his doctrine), that the entire sanctification and pardon of man has its ground not in what he originates within himself, but in what he obtains from God."— *Tholuck on the Romans.*

*grace received from Him which saved them from sin, and was
not of themselves. He perfected His own work in them, through
and by faith, and justified them and sanctified them. . . .
They overcame the enemies of their souls, and him who had the
power of death, by the blood of Him who is Eternal, who is
Jesus the Mediator of the new and living way."*

Francis Howgill's faith was strongly tried, but he
realised that though the power of the enemy is mighty
the power of God is almighty; to His care he entrusted not only himself but also the little Church
of which he was a member, and which was then
enduring a fiery persecution. *Holiness unto the Lord*
was the banner it fearlessly unfurled—not as a mere
motto to be admired, but as setting forth a present
victory by faith over all that is contrary to the will
of God—and therefore it was hated as much by
nominal and lukewarm Christians as by the worldly.
The sufferings of his brethren weighed heavily on
Francis Howgill's heart, which yet was comforted by
the conviction that his fervent prayers for them
would be answered. But he greatly desired to be
able to give them also an assurance of the ultimate
victory that would be theirs, as faithful followers
of Him who goes forth conquering and to conquer;
for

> " The world cannot withstand
> Its ancient Conqueror;
> The world must sink beneath His hand
> Who arms us for the war."

One day whilst he was waiting upon the Lord he
received a remarkable visitation of heavenly love, and
it was clearly shown him that the Lord would deliver
His people though the powers of darkness and of hell
combined against them. He writes, " My heart was
ravished with joy unspeakable; and I was out of the
body with God in His heavenly paradise, where I saw
and felt things unutterable and beyond all demonstration or speech."

In .1661 when writing to Margaret Fell, Francis Howgill says :—" Let me tell thee I am no more weary than the first day the sickle was put into the harvest, when we went out sowing the seed weeping and in tears ; but seeing sheaves brought home and full loads into the barn, and full draughts caught in the net, it hath made me look beyond fainting,— blessed be the Lord ! . . . In Him who is become a place of broad rivers and streams unto us, do I most dearly salute thee." It was in this year that Francis Howgill was imprisoned in London on the false accusation of being engaged in the insurrection of the Fifth Monarchy men.

In the following year a trial of another kind befell him in the loss of his beloved friend and fellow-labourer, Edward Burrough, who, in his twenty-eighth year, died in Newgate, a victim to the pestilential air of a loathsome and frightfully crowded gaol, where the vilest felons were his companions. In a beautiful pathetic testimony to his memory Francis Howgill alludes to the heaven-given strength imparted to Edward Burrough during the wonderful ten years in which he accomplished the work of a lifetime :—

" I know tears were wiped away from thy eyes, because there was no cause, of sorrow in thee ; for I know thou witnessedst the old things done away. And there was no curse, but blessings were poured upon thy head as rain, and peace as a mighty shower. And trouble was far from thy dwelling, though in the outward man trouble on every side ; . . . and now thou art freed from the temptations of him that had the power of death ; and art freed from thy outward enemies who hated thee because of the life that dwelt in thee, . . . and *thy life shall enter into others to testify unto the same Truth which is from everlasting to everlasting.*"

In 1663, when Francis Howgill was one day engaged in business at Kendal, he was arrested in the Market, and brought before the bench of magistrates. They could charge him with no breach of the law, but well knowing that for conscience' sake he could not swear, they designedly tendered him the Oath of Allegiance. This he of course refused to take, and was thereupon committed to Appleby gaol. At the assizes he received the sentence of imprisonment for life, and the forfeiture of his goods and chattels to the king. Turning from the bar he said, "A hard sentence for my obedience to the commands of Christ. The Lord forgive you all!" When the Court broke up there were many who manifested sorrow on his behalf, but he spoke of his gladness in having anything to lose for his Saviour's sake. Thus was he separated from his wife and family, and deprived of liberty for life. Yet blessed is the man who with unswerving loyalty can say :—

> "For THEE my heart has never
> A trustless 'Nay!'"

The patient resignation and loving spirit of the prisoner won the hearts of the gaoler and his whole family, as well as of many others in Appleby ; and such confidence was reposed in him that differences were brought to him for settlement. Debarred from preaching he made diligent use of his pen in writing doctrinal pieces, or in replying to some of the numerous works of the day which wholly misrepresented the principles of Friends. To one of the many epistles which he wrote to those with whom he was united in religious fellowship, the following words are subjoined :—"From Appleby gaol, the place of my rest, where my days and hours are pleasant unto me." When any allusion was made to the length of time that he had been confined he was wont to reply, "The will of the Lord be done."

After an imprisonment of five years and a-half Francis Howgill died, in the fiftieth year of his age. He said that he was ready to die, and praised God for the sweet enjoyment and refreshments he had received,

freely forgiving all who were accountable for his
captivity. The mayor and other of the chief inhabitants of the town came to visit him in his last
illness; and when some of them prayed that God
would speak peace to his soul, he gently replied "He
hath done it." When, a few hours before his death,
some friends came to see him he fervently prayed for
them that the Lord "by His mighty power might
preserve them out of all such things as would spot or
defile." "If any man inquire about my latter end,"
he said, "let them know that I die in the faith which
I lived in and suffered for." His death occurred in
the latter part of 1663.

"*As man cometh to believe in His strength unto
whom all power is committed, the covenant with death
is broken, . . . and so the creature comes to be
delivered from the bondage of corruption.*" Thus, in
words which might well serve for an exposition of
2 Pet. i. 4, did Francis Howgill write, in his clear
comprehension of the completeness of Christ's redemption, and the boundlessness of His grace. That grace
which is freely offered, and all-sufficient for those who
without waiting for any special state of feeling, cease
from struggling and self-preparation, and lay hold of
it in the exercise of that true and simple faith with
which is ever blended the desire for entire conformity
to the will of God; yielding themselves wholly to Him
who was "wounded for our transgressions," opening
every avenue of the soul, in order that they may be
filled with His Spirit. The more fully this grace is
trusted in, and the more deeply it is proved—whilst
completely renouncing all self-dependence—the more
shall we give to God of "glory" (Rom. iv. 20), and
realise that He is able to make all grace abound"
towards us that we "may abound to every good
work" (2 Cor. ix. 8).

III.

SAMUEL WATSON AND ROGER HEBDEN.

" HAVE you ever known an instance in which our Heavenly Father has failed the man who trusted absolutely in Him, and gave himself up, heart and soul to His will? . . . Give yourselves absolutely to God, and there is no such thing as questioning whether or no He has the power to uphold."

DR. TEMPLE, *Bishop of Exeter.*

SAMUEL WATSON AND ROGER HEBDEN.

" And they are walking with Me still,
　Who follow after good and hate the ill,
　And who, for love of Me, My law of love fulfil.

" And what I darkly spake before,
　I will unfold more clearly evermore,
　The future and the past, and all divinest lore.

" Then what though trouble never cease ?
　What though the waves that buffet you increase ?
　The world is at My feet, in Me ye shall have peace."

R. C.

" In the latter days these things shall be considered more perfectly ; " so wrote Samuel Watson some 200 years ago in his " Testimony of God's Power." " The operation of true faith," he remarks in this little book, "is when thou feelest Christ's love and power stripping thee of thy old garment of sin and filthy rags, which is thy own righteousness received by tradition, and comes to clothe thee with innocency. So that now, through His blood, who is the Lamb of God, thou art washed from the spots of uncleanness and natural corruption . . . Thou art brought to confess that Christ Jesus is come into the world, thy Saviour, to save thee from thy sins."

Samuel Watson's home was at Knight-Stainforth, in Yorkshire, and the family from which he was descended was esteemed one of the chief in the parish. When he was about the age of thirty-four some demands were made on the estate that came to him from his father, which he deemed so unjust that he chose to suffer imprisonment rather than yield to them. And thus it came to pass that he formed the

acquaintance of Thomas Aldam and several other
Friends who were confined in York Castle for the non-
payment of tithes. Samuel Watson—who, whilst by
no means indifferent to religion, was in an unsettled
state of mind with regard to it—gladly embraced the
opportunity for holding converse with them.

In this time of withdrawal from active life he also
read some of the writings of Friends. Above all, he
searched the Scriptures, and learning that "nothing
would avail but a new creature," he yielded humbly
and fully to the powerful visitation of the Holy Spirit.
By the blood of Christ his conscience was "purged
from dead works to serve the *living* God," for as such
he knew Him now. Frivolous worldly pastimes and
formal ways of worship were alike forsaken, and he
found that the Lord, to whom he had dedicated himself, was calling him to the blessed service of pro-
claiming liberty to captive souls. He therefore took
measures to regain his freedom by making an agree-
ment with respect to the disputed liability.

The imprisonment of his Friend, *Thomas Aldam,*
lasted for two years and a-half. Thomas Aldam, his
wife, and two sisters, were among the first converts of
George Fox in Yorkshire. His ministry was the means
of teaching Thomas Aldam that his longings for
holiness need not remain unsatisfied ; and one of our
chroniclers tells us, "he, having received the Truth,
was valiant for the same upon earth, and gave up his
strength and substance to serve the Lord."

Thomas Aldam was one of the first Friends who was
a prisoner for conscience' sake in York Castle ; he
was not even once allowed to go to his home, nor see
any of his children, and was sometimes refused an
interview with his wife when she came to visit him.
Meanwhile a clergyman sued him treble damages for
the non-payment of tithes, taking from him property
to the value of £58 10s.—no trifling sum in those

days—not leaving one cow to supply his little children with milk. This clergyman also threatened to deprive the family of a cow which had been lent them by a relative.

In 1654, the year of his liberation, Thomas Aldam was one day going to see some of his imprisoned friends at York, when as he approached the door of the prison he was attacked by some low, rough men, who struck him, stoned him, and threw water at him. A magistrate was standing by whilst all this went on, but the only use he made of his office was to commit Thomas Aldam to prison as the author of the uproar. Nor was this by any means the sole occasion on which he met with violent abuse. Once at Rosington, the churchwarden having given him a blow on the cheek, he literally turned the other to him ; for like George Fox, his spiritual father, he might have said, " the spirit of strife is slain within me."

Thomas Aldam's first imprisonment in York Castle was followed by at least three more. The fervency of his spirit left a deep impression on the mind of his son, who says that before his father left home on the Lord's service, he would call his family around him, and kneeling down would commend them to God's safe keeping, and ask for His continued presence with himself ; at these times many tears were shed, not of sorrow, but because their hearts were melted by the sense of God's great love and goodness ;—

> " God's love so walls us round about
> How is it possible to doubt ?"

Thomas Aldam visited all or most of the goals in England, and some of those in Scotland and Ireland, in which his brethren were confined, for the sake of laying before Oliver Cromwell authentic proof of the exceeding extent of the persecution to which Friends were subjected.

Of his wife, Mary Aldam, we are told that she served the Lord, and was " of a very meek and quiet spirit, given up in all things to God's disposing ;" so it is not surprising that a writer of the*following generation should say : " Her remembrance is sweet, and her name to be recorded amongst the faithful of God's people."

We must now see how it fared with Samuel Watson, the current of whose life was turned into a new channel during his intercourse with Thomas Aldam and the other Friends who were his fellow-prisoners in York Castle.   One who knew him well for many years says that a wonderful change was seen in him, which much surprised his acquaintance, who marvelled that a man in his position should abandon such things as they thought most worth living for, and should throw open his house as a meeting-place for Friends.   But he had loyally given his heart to ONE who has infinite power to bless, but whose kingdom is not of this world.

> " Count me a fool, O world ! to loose
>   My hands from holding fast thy gains—
> A little while if there I choose,
>   The hands are dust, and what remains ?
>
> " Count me a fool ! mine eyes to close,
>   Save to the things I cannot see ;
> Thine are the shadows, cheats and shows,
>   That pass, and change, and seem to be."*

He established meetings . in several towns, and travelled diligently in the work of the ministry, amidst varied persecution from scoffing, stoning, stocks, blows and imprisonment.   Bold and resolute as was his spirit, Samuel Watson bore all this with unfailing patience.

---

* Isa Craig Knox.

It seems to have been no very rare event in those days for a layman to address a congregation at the end of the usual service, and one day Samuel Watson made an attempt to speak in the church of Giggles-worth. But he was thrown down with violence, and after his head had been struck against the seats, he was dragged out of the church and flung down on the ice. At Leeds under similar circumstances he fared somewhat better, for there he did not encounter personal violence, but was imprisomed for eight days in a cell, without anything to lie on.

At another time when Samuel Watson was at a meeting of Friends at Burton, in Bishop's Dale, it was broken up by a constable and some rough men, who sorely abused the quiet worshippers. One man, armed with a staff and pistol, threatened to fire at Samuel Watson, and struck him so violently that it was at first supposed he was really killed. As soon as he had sufficiently recovered he was hurried off to the stocks.

In 1660 Samuel Watson was one of two hundred and twenty-nine persons who were committed to prison, in the course of November and December, for refusing to take the Oath. Some were arrested whilst quietly sitting in a meeting, some whilst walking on the high road, some whilst engaged in business; others were taken from their beds. During this imprisonment Samuel Watson wrote a letter to the Friends residing in and around York, from which the following extract is taken :—

"The Sun of Righteousness will arise . . . if you faint not, with healing in His wings, and the shadows will flee away, and the powerful circumcision in spirit will be felt in you. . . . That which was and is my strength shall be thy strength, to give victory over thine enemies, and in the over-coming life thou wilt rejoice. . . . And thou who comes to this, the name of the Lord is as precious ointment in thee, which keeps thee fresh and living, offering up a spiritual sacrifice in thy holy breathings unto Him."

Then he presses on his friends the duty of attending meetings :—

"The Lord would not have you lukewarm, lest He withdraw your present mercies . . . and if there should not be any to speak publicly it may *sometimes* be for your good. . . . As you keep to the watch you know not in what a wonderful manner the Lord in His love may meet with you. *He delights in this, that you draw near unto Him with a true heart in full assurance to partake of His love;* and I am a witness His hand is open to fill thee who thus comes unto Him. . . . Likewise how do you know, as you are kept in the watching, but the Lord may pour out His spirit of prayer and supplication, *upon you, and give you an understanding to utter words before Him to His glory and to the edification of others?* Hear the voice of Christ speaking in you as ever He did to His disciples : 'Could ye not watch *with me* one hour ? ' "

Near the close of another letter written to his friends at this time he says :—

"Wait to feel the spiritual union when our bodies are separate one from another, wherein the blessing of the Lord will be all, and in all of you enjoyed."

Samuel Watson was again imprisoned in 1682, and two years later we find his signature, with that of sixteen other Friends, in an address to Charles II., on behalf of themselves and two hundred and thirteen other prisoners confined in the county gaol of York. This document briefly states the cause and manner of their committal, the hardships which some of them had endured, and the grievous spoil which had been made of their property. The whole value of the goods which had been seized amounted to £1,509, almost a fortune two hundred years ago, and yet the mere figures by no means show the suffering caused by these distraints. The bailiffs had taken the very bed from under the sick, and had almost ruined families by depriving workmen of their tools, and farmers of their implements. Some of the prisoners had been prosecuted for non-attendance at church, and others for holding meetings in their houses.

It was during this imprisonment, which seems to have lasted for three years or longer, that Samuel Watson wrote a pamphlet entitled, "A Testimony of the Regenerate"; a few passages from which follow :—

"Oh blessed Father," he begins, "how great is Thy love, and how gracious Thy visitations unto my immortal soul! Now do I hear Thy voice in the still calm manifestation of Thy ancient love, wherein Thou madest known Thyself unto the patriarchs of old; though after divers manners Thou spake unto them, yet it was in the same power and the same Spirit of the Son . . . and through the virtue of the blood of the spotless Lamb which suffered death upon the cross, through the one offering in the Eternal Spirit, Thou hast purged my conscience from dead works and dead sacrifices, and hast washed and cleansed my garments. . . . And not only so, but translated me into the glorious light and liberty of Thy Son. . . . Can I take up my rest in any polluted path? . . . Surely, Father, Thou hast come near unto me with the circumcision of Thine own Spirit."

Then, after an allusion to the time when, " for want of living faith," he could not get the victory over the world, he continues, "Thy will be done in earth as it is in heaven, for *Thou hast subdued my will which ruled by nature unto Thy heavenly will which is my sanctification.*" These last few words recall that sweet old hymn of the fourteenth century :—

> "Even as now my hands
> So doth my folded will
> Lie waiting Thy commands
> Without one anxious thrill.

> "Nothing but perfect trust
> And love of Thy perfect will
> Can raise me out of the dust,
> And bid my fears be still."*

---

* David Nasmith, the founder of Town Missions, when in feeble health went on his Master's work to Guildford. There, away from

In a treatise written by Samuel Watson during an earlier imprisonment in York Castle, we find the following passages :—

"From the days of John the Baptist until now, the kingdom of Heaven suffereth violence, and the violent take it by force. But if through *fervent love* thou wouldst enter the kingdom (thou professing Christian), thou must forsake the world and have a fervent zeal after righteousness. . . . *Man's striving in his will cannot do it, but through faith in Jesus Christ the overcoming is.* . . . He illuminates, He opens the heart, He sanctifieth. . . . This is He in whom I believe and who is my Saviour, in and through whose precious blood is my salvation and redemption."

One of Samuel Watson's fellow-prisoners was *John Blaikling*, of Draw-well, in the parish of Sedbergh, to whom, with his wife and father and mother, George Fox had been the bearer of the glad tidings of a free and full salvation, in 1652. They joyfully received him as their guest, and John Blaikling was his companion in his memorable meeting at Firbank Chapel. John Blaikling became a minister, and travelled extensively in England and Scotland on this service. He was a man of sound judgment and of deep experience in heavenly lore ; a warm encourager of those who believed that the Lord was calling them to speak in His name ; a peacemaker, and an unselfish helper of such as were in need. At the time of his death he had nearly reached his eightieth year. In a last letter to one of his friends he writes, " I love thee in the truest love that springs from Jesus Christ, the fountain thereof, by and in which my life standeth. I am

---

his beloved wife and children, " amid sudden disease and excruciating agony he died at an inn. One Christian brother alone, who had received a letter of introduction by his hands, witnessing his end." This gentleman said to him, " It is hard amid such trouble as this to say ; ' The Lord's will be done ; ' " but he replied with energy, " *Not at all !*"

almost blind, yet well content." When taking leave of his intimate friend, Thomas Camm, with many tears and warm embraces, John Blaikling spoke of how if they never saw one another again in this life, yet in eternity their spirits, with the spirits of just men made perfect, "*should meet never to part again.*" " I pray God with all my soul," he added, " if it be His will for His truth and people's sake, to lengthen thy days."

Samuel Watson had the sorrow, in 1688, of losing a young daughter, at the age of nineteen, a trial the more keenly felt by himself and her mother because of her absence from them in London at the time of her death. " A sweet, beautiful child," her father calls her. When only about ten years of age her mother, when talking to her one day, said, " I have fought the good fight of faith, and a crown of glory is laid up for me." These words made so deep an impression on little Grace's mind that shortly before her death she told her sister she had never forgotten them, and added, " *I* can now say, ' I finish my course with joy, and shall receive a crown of glory.'" " Oh! Heavenly Father, what hast Thou done for me this night !" was her exclamation on another occasion ; " how hast Thou removed the crooked serpent ! . . . Thou hast shone in upon me with Thy marvellous light. Thou hast showed me the glory of Thy house, . . . Thou hast made my cup to run over, over, over ! How can I cease praising Thee, Thou God of power ? " Indeed, the clear consciousness of the love of her reconciled Father in heaven strengthend that warm young heart willingly to resign the friends she so fondly loved. Taking her sister by the hand, she said, " Though we be separated outwardly, we shall meet in the kingdom of glory."

Samuel Watson does not record the date of the death of his daughter, Mary Moss, of Manchester, nor state the age at which she was called away from her husband and young children :—

"It was not that their love was cold
That earthly lights were burning dim,
But that the Shepherd from His fold
Had smiled and drawn her unto Him."

" *Great in love,*" her father says, " but little in her
own eyes, a handmaid of the Lord manifesting her love
and the law of kindness to all, . . . many have been
comforted in those springs of life that streamed from
that well of salvation opened in her."* It is plain
that she was one of those who

" For love of Christ, His law of love fulfil;"

thus she would rather silently suffer much than make
known the faults of others. " I can now leave her,"
writes Samuel Watson, " in the arms of her blessed
Saviour, at whose feet she kept in the days of her
pilgrimage, and washed them spritually with the tears
of joy." And then he reminds his readers that they
are not their own, but " bought with a price." "A
holy engagement is upon you to serve the Lord in
your souls, bodies, and spirits, which are His."

But it was in 1694, fourteen years before his own
death, that Samuel Watson's heaviest trial befell him
in the loss of his wife, who had been not only a most
beloved companion and fellow-labourer in the Gospel,
but bound to him by the closest ties of spiritual
sympathy. Together they had passed through many
exercises of soul; together they had poured out their
hearts in prayer to the God who had been their
strength in the day of trouble, and who had shed
abroad His love in their hearts, and had satisfied their
souls with the hidden manna.

During Mary Watson's last illness she often spoke
of being surrounded by the glory of the Lamb of God.

---

* John iv. 14, and vii. 38, 39.

A few hours before her peaceful end she said to her husband, as she had often been wont to do, " Love, pray for me." " The *never-failing* sacrifice which God prepares," Samuel Watson says, " sprang up in me, which the Lord, our tender Heavenly Father, hath heard and answered." He adds that she died " in a sweet, still manner ; . . . and now I am left in separation from her visible body, but *I am still with her in a spiritual union in the heavenly place.*"

The last years of Samuel Watson's life were spent at Chester, at the house of his son-in-law ; he died in the year 1708, at the age of eighty-eight.

Samuel Watson twice visited the meetings of Friends in Scotland, and on the first of these occasions a minister named Roger Hebden was his companion. At the time of George Fox's remarkable visit to Yorkshire, in 1651, Roger Hebden was thirty years of age, and was employed in keeping a draper's shop at Malton. In childhood and early youth he had often been conscience-smitten for some wandering from the path of duty, but, notwithstanding this and his frequent attendance at religious services, had failed to discover that God was dealing with him, until the very depths of his soul were stirred by the heaven-given message of George Fox. Then the fervent desire arose in his heart to choose God for his portion, and yield entire obedience to Him ; but he was weighed down by the burden of past sin until the Holy Spirit brought home to his soul the inspired words, " Though your sins be as scarlet they shall be as white as snow ; though they be red like crimson they shall be as wool ; " " whereupon," he says, " I found peace, this condition being concluded upon—to be obedient unto Him for the time to come. This was the day of the Lord's great power."

The mighty hand of a God of love was upon him, and he had no wish to resist it. And now his heart was melted with sorrow when he was led to see how

long he had closed it against the Lord, who had laid
down His life for him. " Born again ! " " a new
creature ! " were the words which seemed to ring in
his ears, " which condition," he adds, " is now witnessed." His sorrow was turned into joy ; and he goes
on to say : " About six months after the Lord poured
forth His spirit of prayer and prophecy upon me.
Thus I came to be made a minister of Christ, whom I
preach."

His labours were the means of turning many to
righteousness. The Friends of his Monthly Meeting
record that " as his doctrine was godly, so his conversation was blameless ; " and state that his ministry,
though often of a consoling character, was " sharp,
powerful, and penetrating, and wanted not its triumph."
The free use of Scriptural illustration was one of its
most marked features.* Some of the more serious
folk of Malton would eagerly ask when Roger Hebden
would be at the meeting there.

In a " Testimony," signed by a dozen friends of his,
after a reference to the blessed effects of his ministry,
it is remarked that they need say the less " as to his
innocent life and blameless conversation," because he
was so well known, not only to the members of his
own Society, but to all those who dwelt thereabouts,

---

* " We are *absolutely dependent* on the Lord of the harvest, but
the hand of the diligent maketh rich. The instructed scribe was
the copier of Scripture, and therefore was supposed to be intimately
acquainted with it. Our kind Master would dwell in a well-
furnished house, where all things are in their place. Therefore
Paul tells Timothy not only that the Scriptures are able to make
wise unto salvation, through faith which is in Christ Jesus, but he
further tells him that all Scripture given by inspiration of God is
profitable, ' that the man of God may be perfect, throughly *furnished* unto all good works.' Paul's figure is not an empty vessel.
but a purged ' vessel unto honour, sanctified and meet for the
Master's use, prepared unto every good work.' "—*Henry Stanley
Newman.*

for many miles around, "which was," they quaintly add, "one means to make his public testimony abundantly more acceptable." They also allude to his apt quotation of Scripture for the sake of clearly demonstrating the truths he dwelt on.

And they write of his *tenderness* in dealing with the ignorant and the wanderer; that element which can hardly be thought too much of in soul-winning. The new heart is said to be "a heart of flesh," and therefore a heart warm, loving, and full of sympathy. To God alone belongs the power to raise the physically or the spiritually dead. He could have brought back life to the Shunamite's son by means of the prophet's staff; but it was not His will so to do. The staff was indeed laid on the face of the child, but "there was neither voice nor hearing," and Elisha was told, "The child is not awaked." Nor was there an awakening from that sleep of death until the prophet "stretched himself upon the child, and put his mouth upon his mouth, and his eyes upon his eyes, and his hands upon his hands."*

One of Roger Hebden's personal friends, after a reference to George Fox's visit to Yorkshire, records how God's Spirit was poured out on Roger Hebden, so that he, with many more of us, could say to our great satisfaction and joy, "*The Lord hath spoken, who can keep silent!*" As Roger Hebden had an estate of his own he now made it his residence, giving up his business at Malton to another Friend. He travelled as a minister at his own expense, and established meetings in various places. He had married in early life, and his wife was a true helpmeet.

---

* "The great secret of helping others is to come down as Christ came down, to make yourself of no reputation . . . go down, *get underneath them, and lift them up.*"—*Hay Macdonald Grant, of Arndilly.*

Roger Hebden's first imprisonment was the not-to-be-wondered at result of his plain-speaking in the church at Newton, apparently at the conclusion of the usual sermon.   A constable was committed to prison at the same time because, when bidden by a magistrate to take Roger Hebden to gaol, he had answered, " I will not; I had rather be a sufferer than a persecutor."

" I am in their hands," wrote Roger Hebden, " but at liberty in the spirit of the Lord!"   One of the letters written during this imprisonment was addressed to his brother, John Hebden, and from it the following extract is taken :—

" Time was when Paul found a law in his members warring against the law in his mind, . . . and then he cried out in his wretchedness.   But he here did not rest himself satisfied, as the professors of the world now do, who take this condition of his—when he cried out under the burden of his misery and in his warfare—to plead for a hold for sin in them as long as they live ; but he looks up to Christ and thanks God that He gave him the victory *through Him*, . . . which condition is now witnessed, the conquest gotten by the same Conqueror."

In a letter to his friends at Malton he desires that they may know " a growth in the vine from which the knitting and uniting of hearts comes."

Roger Hebden rejoiced in the communion of saints, but remarks that receiving bread and wine together does not unite us into one.   He also says that when he did take the sacrament, although he had thirsted to receive something of Christ at the same time, he had come empty away.   Then he learnt that the communion which would satisfy his soul was a supping with Christ; and the baptism which would meet his need was the pouring out of God's Spirit upon him.

The Conventicle Act, passed in 1614, pressed with especial severity on Friends, as it made it unlawful for more than five persons, who were not members of the same household, to assemble for religious worship otherwise than in accordance with the book of Common Prayer. But no threats of fines, imprisonment or banishment could hinder Roger Hebden from worshipping God in the manner he believed to be right.

Soon after the passing of this Act, Roger Hebden was present at a meeting at Sherif-Hutton ; with a deep sense of God's goodness to His people, he had knelt down to offer vocal prayer, when a man, who was accompanied by some soldiers, rushed into the quiet assembly, and, laying violent hands on him, took him before Sir Thomas Gowre, who was a magistrate. He asked Roger Hebden if he had spoken in the meeting, and on receiving his reply told him that he had transgressed the Act. Roger Hebden's wife was standing by, and, self-forgetful in her loyalty to him and to their common Lord, felt well content—as she afterwards told him—that if his prayer were a transgression of the Act he should suffer for it. He was confined in York Castle for more than eleven weeks.

Another imprisonment took place early in the following year, when he was taken from a meeting at Bishop's Wilton, and, with nineteen other Friends, committed to York Castle for three months. "The prosecutors of this Act," he writes, "who thought to have wearied us, grew weary in many places, and Truth prevailed exceedingly. Blessed be the Lord for ever, whose work it is to strengthen His, and to give them courage and comfort every way."

Roger Hebden died in 1695, at the age of seventy-five. No particulars of his last days appear to be left on record for us, but we are told in few and simple, yet forcible, words, that "as he lived so he died."

The lives of such men point their own moral. They dedicated themselves to God, and the "good pleasure of His goodness and the work of faith with power was fulfilled in them." But no less truly may the Lord be served by many "whose history never arrested human observation, who never bare the name of martyrs, but who early offering themselves to Christ were silently accepted by Him, and in secret places, unknown to the world, have been 'taught in suffering' what they were one day to 'teach in song.' Perhaps they are not shown in this life the countless souls they have lifted out of the dust, or elevated above the ordinary plane of existence. But long before they go home to their reward, 'there shall be no night' in the celestial city of their souls."*

* Mrs. Prentiss.

IV.

JOSEPH COALE AND AMBROSE RIGGE.

" Count me o'er earth's chosen heroes,—they were souls that
  stood alone,
  While the men they agonized for hurled the contumelious
  stone,
  Stood serene, and down the future saw the golden beam
  incline
  To the side of perfect justice, mastered by their faith divine.

  .   .   .   .

" Tis as easy to be heroes as to sit the idle slaves
  Of a legendary virtue carved upon our fathers' graves ;
  Worshippers of light ancestral make the present light a
  crime ;—
  Was the *Mayflower* launched by cowards, steered by men
  behind their time ?
  Turn those tracks toward Past or Future that make
  Plymouth Rock sublime ?

" They were men of present valour, stalwart old iconoclasts,
  Unconvinced by axe or gibbet that all virtue was the Past's.
  But we make their truth our falsehood, thinking that has
  set us free,
  Hoarding it in mouldy parchments while our tender spirits
  flee
  The rude grasp of that great Impulse which drove them
  across the sea."

James Russell Lowell.

JOSEPH COALE AND AMBROSE RIGGE.

"The Law promised a crown when the struggle was over.   Grace *first* crowned and then led the soldier to battle."

CHRYSOSTOM *on Rom.* vi. 14.

IN the spring of 1670 a young man lay dying in Reading gaol.   His health had broken down in consequence of an imprisonment of six years' duration, the penalty for his conscientious refusal to take the Oath of Allegiance; for, in common with his brethren in religious fellowship, he yielded literal obedience to Christ's injunction—"Swear not at all," believing that whatsoever is more than Yea and Nay cometh of evil; of that evil from which they had been redeemed by Christ.   When addressing the friends who were gathered around him, he said: "The light of that glorious everlasting day of the Lord which has broken forth in this our day shall never be extinguished, notwithstanding all that man can do.   And though it may be in the hearts of men to destroy and root out (if it were possible) the righteous from off the earth, yet the Lord doth not intend so, neither is it in His heart to suffer it so to be, but to exalt His own Name and Kingdom over all.*

---

* About a century later, as Joseph White, an American minister of the Society of Friends, lay dying, he said, "I have for some time believed—and am now in measure confirmed—of more glorious things yet to be revealed to the Church of Christ, and that further and greater discoveries will be made with respect to the Christian religion than have been since the apostasy.   I cannot utter what I feel of that light, life, and love!"

This young man was Joseph Coale, who, at the age of nineteen, had been one of the first in Berkshire to cast in his lot with the Friends, when that county was visited by some earnest ministers. Not long afterwards he found himself a prisoner, but was liberated through the exertions of the person to whom he was apprenticed. Called to the ministry of the Word, thus early began those afflictions of the Gospel of which during the remainder of his life he was so largely to partake. But God had not given him "the spirit of fear, but of power and of love and of a sound mind," and he was not ashamed of the testimony of his Lord.

In the following year, 1656, at the expiration of his apprenticeship, Joseph Coale went to Cornwall, in order to visit the Friends who were enduring a cruel confinement there.

The place into which the gaoler had thrust George Fox and his companions was one in which murderers were wont to be confined. Few who entered it ever came out again in health, for it was—and for some years had been—in a state of loathsomeness which defies description. Some said that the place was haunted, hoping perhaps to arouse the prisoners' terror. "But I told them," says George Fox, "that if all the spirits and devils in hell were there, I was over them all in the power of God, and feared no such thing. For Christ, our Priest, would sanctify the walls and the house to us ; He who bruised the head of the devil, . . . who sanctifies both inwardly and outwardly the walls of the house, the walls of the heart, and all things to His people."

Joseph Coale, yearning to alleviate the sufferings of these prisoners, solicited an interview with Justice Nichols, taking with him a letter from George Fox. Some of the more serious people of the town who came to visit the captives had become their converts, and this aroused great rage among the nominal professors of religion and the ministers. One of these visitors was a young gentleman, aged twenty-four, belonging to an ancient Cornish family of the name of Lower, whose interest and curiosity had probably been awakened by all that he had heard about George Fox. He generously offered the prisoners money, which they refused, whilst responding to the love which had prompted the proposal. He put many questions to them on religious subjects, and George Fox spoke particularly to him. Thomas Lower afterwards remarked that George Fox's words were as a flash of lightning running through him. He had never met with such men, he said, for they knew the thoughts of his heart, and were as the wise master-builders of assemblies who fastened their words like nails.

Thomas Lower became a Friend, and soon afterwards married Elizabeth, daughter of Sir John Trelawny, Baronet. George Fox's ministry had been a heaven-sent message to her, in a meeting held at the house of a gentleman who resided at Plymouth. Six years after her early death, Thomas Lower became the husband of George Fox's stepdaughter, Mary Fell. He was sometimes George Fox's companion in his ministerial journeys, and on one occasion shared his imprisonment in Worcester gaol, where they were confined on the plea that they " held meetings upon the pretence of the exercise of religion otherwise than is established by the laws of England." After some time had elapsed, they laid the case before Lord Windsor, the lord-lieutenant of the county, but without success. A letter with regard to Thomas Lower's liberation was, however, addressed to Lord Windsor by a brother of his at Court, apparently at the request of Dr. Richard Lower, who was physician to the King and brother of Thomas Lower. But as no mention was made of George Fox in this letter which was sent

under cover to Thomas Lower, such was his loving
loyalty to his father in the truth that he did not present it to the lord-lieutenant.

But we must go back to the year of their first acquaintance at Launceston, when Joseph Coale's efforts
for the release of one of the prisoners, and for the relief
of all from the cruelty of the gaoler, were unheeded by
Justice Nichols. Yet he made out a mittimus for
Joseph Coale himself, and sent him as a vagrant to
Launceston gaol, where he was confined for many
months. As soon as he was set at liberty Joseph
Coale turned his face westwards in order to visit the
Cornish Friends ; but as he was quietly pursuing his
solitary way, on a part of the lonely high road that
crossed the pleasant, breezy downs, he was met by a
Major Ceely who apprehended him, and he was again
committed, as " a wanderer," to Launceston gaol, where
he spent three months more.

When he at length reached the west of Cornwall he
went one day with some other Friends to "a meeting
for the worship of God," which had been appointed at
Penryhn. But this peaceful assembly was roughly
broken up by Captain Fox, the governor of Pendennis
Castle, who came with a troop of horse, and violently
abused some of the quiet worshippers. Perhaps this
meeting had been held at the request of Joseph Coale,
who seems to have been the marked victim of Captain
Fox's malice. The loss of blood caused by the treatment he received was so great that his friends at first
feared it would cost him his life. In his visit to the
quaint, picturesque old seaport of Fowey, he was
accompanied by Thomas Lower, whose acquaintance
he had no doubt made during his imprisonment at
Launceston. Joseph Coale preached in the streets
and market-place of Fowey, and stones were thrown
at him and his companion as they left the town.

When at Exeter a few weeks later, Joseph Coale

went into a church to exhort the people to repentance. In those days laymen occasionally addressed the congregation at the conclusion of the usual service. But some of those present soon laid hands on him; he was taken to the town-hall, and thence to the gaol, where we are told that he was confined in a very filthy place; strong words, which nevertheless seem scarcely strong enough for the description of its state. For the High Gaol of Exeter has been styled, by an author who had no sympathy with Friends,—" a living tomb, a sink of filth, pestilence, and profligacy." Indeed at the time traditionally termed the " Black Assizes," some prisoners bearing with them into the Court the taint of the terrible gaol fever, Sergeant Flowerby, the presiding judge, five of the magistrates, and eleven of the jury, straightway sickened and died. As much later as the days of John Howard, the surgeon was excused in his contract from visiting any prisoners in the dungeons who were suffering from that frightful pestilence.*

Orders were given that Joseph Coale should have a heavy pair of double irons fastened to one of his legs, and that he should be allowed neither bed nor straw to lie on. The next week, after being threatened, he was set at liberty.†

About four years later, when again at Exeter, Joseph Coale was taken out of a meeting for worship,

---

* *Early Records of Friends in Devonshire.*

† In an old Devonshire Monthly Meeting book is the following entry drawn up for transmission to London. " EXON.—The first yᵗ came in yᵉ testimony of truth to this place was Geo. Fox, who had a meeting at one Morgin's, at yᵉ sine of yᵉ Seven Starres neare Ex. Bridge, where were several of Plymouth and Kingsbridge Friends." The Seven Stars Inn still stands at the foot of the bridge which connects Exter with St. Thomas.

and, the Oath of Allegiance having been tendered him
in vain, was again imprisoned in the gaol for three
months.   The well-known objection of the Friends to
even judicial swearing was terribly taken advantage of
by their persecutors. In one of Joseph Coale's writings,
after stating the ground of the refusal of Friends to
take the oath, he adds, "Therefore upon this general
account we cannot swear allegiance to the king, but we
can and have proffered to promise in faithfulness, and
do desire that the same punishment may be inflicted
upon those that break their word and promise, as on
them that break their oaths. . . . It is a common saying among men, ' *Those that will swear will lie*'! . . .
If it had been known that ever we could swear in any
case since we were a people, and would not now swear
allegiance to the king, then, indeed, there were great
cause of suspicion.   We have always desired the good
and happiness of the king and all men in this world
and that which is to come!"

In *those* days, when the fact of "not having written
a book" could hardly have been called "a distinc-
tion," the multiplicity of the writings of many of the
prominent early Friends was remarkable, notwithstanding the activity of their lives and the frequent
journeys performed, with none of the facilities of
modern travel.   Whilst some of these authors wrote
chiefly for the sake of refuting the calumnies of those
who hated or misunderstood them, with others it
would seem that their souls so overflowed with living
water that preaching alone did not suffice them, and
their pens became the pens of ready writers, because
they *could not* hide God's righteousness within their
hearts.   Moreover, not unfrequently close confinement
in dreary dungeons necessitated writing, if they would
declare to others God's faithfulness and His salvation.

Although Joseph Coale's works are far less numerous
than those of many of his brethren, they give ample

proof of his realisation of the fulness and complete-
ness of Christ's salvation.   In his " Testimony of the
Father's Love, after alluding to " the rule and authority which the prince of darkness hath had in the
hearts of men," he adds :—

" Christ destroys that and subdues His enemies that would
not that He should reign.   And who come to know this,
they may say, as one said once, ' The Lord reigneth, let the
earth rejoice.'   Mark—*the Lord reigneth.*   What ! Did the
Lord reign while they were upon the earth ? Yes, while they
were upon the earth ; . . . and darkness was past away, and
sin was blotted out, and herein they rejoiced. . . . Oh ! what
a great profession is in this nation ? And how many do take
the pure name of God and Christ in their mouths, and yet
hate to be reformed. . . . People would reign with Christ
and live with Him after death, as they say, when they can sin
no longer, *then* they would reign with Christ ; but plead for
sin, and say they can never be free from it while they are
here."

Again, in an epistle to the Friends of Henley, we
find the following passage :—

" The light of the morning is sprung up unto you in whose
hearts the day-star is risen, and the darkness is now passing
away, and will pass away more and more with the enjoyment of
the love and peace of God, and into fellowship and union with
Him, and into the knowledge and virtue of the precious blood
of Jesus Christ, *which doth really and truly cleanse and wash
away all sin and uncleanness,* . . . and such as believe in it,
and witness the cleansing by it, do most truly know it.
Elsewhere he says : " You that have known this, oh, Friends !
keep yourselves clean, if you are washed and your garments
are made white in the blood of the Lamb, that you be not
again defiled with the evil of this world."

Joseph Coale's brother records that his Gospel
labours in several places were performed at the hazard
of his life : sometimes as he says, " in prisons, stock-
ings and stonings, hardships and difficulties."   It is
interesting to know that he visited Ireland with

Edward Burrough.   When about the age of twenty-three Joseph Coale was committed to Dorchester gaol for the offences of exhorting people to repentance in the market-place at Lynne, (Lyme Regis); and for preaching in Bridport church.

In this county gaol he found Ambrose Rigge, who was only some two or three years older than himself. Ambrose Rigge writes of the dreadful malady raging there, "which some called the plague," and which "swept away most of the prisoners." But the Lord, he tells us, was with him, keeping him in the hollow of His hand, and during the eleven weeks of his imprisonment he says that he had the joy of performing "very good service for the Lord, to the convincing and confirming of many in the truth in which they have now found rest for their souls."

Thus simply do some of these good men record the manner in which the Lord's blessing had rested on their labours.   It is consistent with their genuine conviction that without Christ they could do nothing.   All their springs were in Him.   It was of His wondrous works they talked or wrote, and to Him they gave the glory.*

Ambrose Rigge writes that the Lord gave him the assurance that not a hair of his head should fall without Him; and he was not only preserved from the fearful disease which swept away many around, but was kept in excellent health.   Thus in that pestilential air, with the dead and dying around him, was he rescued by the hand of Him who of old closed the mouths of the lions for His faithful servant's sake.

---

* "You must take care not to work too much *yourself*. By this I mean that you must look *decidedly* to the Holy Spirit to do the work, and to Him alone. . . . We sometimes are tempted to act as if *we* were doing the work instead of the Holy Spirit."—*Hay Macdowal Grant, of Arndilly.*

And may we not say of him as of Daniel, "No manner of hurt was found on him because he believed in his God"? Humphrey Smith, another Friend who was in the gaol, was brought very near to death, but was raised up again. Ambrose Rigge was his devoted nurse, and he would take nothing but from his hand.

In Berkshire the persecution of Friends was carried on with great violence by William Armourer, a justice of the peace, who not only availed himself to the utmost of the license granted by law in the reign of Charles II., but even exceeded its bounds in his gross abuse of his innocent and peaceful neighbours. He had a particular grudge against one of Joseph Coale's friends, Thomas Curtis, of Reading, at whose house a meeting was now held.

When, on one occasion, Thomas Curtis had been taken from a meeting, instead of being legally tried he was ensnared by the tender of the Oath of Allegiance, and committed to the sheriff's custody. He, however, obtained leave to go to Bristol fair on business; but the news of this being heard by Armourer, he sent for him, and saying, "I hear you are going to Bristol fair, but I will stop your journey," he withdrew him without any legal authority from the sheriff's charge, and confined him in the town gaol. He found some plea also for the imprisonment of the wife, and then of the man-servant, of Thomas Curtis, thus making it necessary that Curtis's shop should be closed. Even the maid-servant was committed to the House of Correction by him for two days and nights.

She had perhaps aroused his anger by her refusal to open the door to him when he came to inquire whether anyone was in the house besides Curtis's family at the time when Joseph Coale was finding a temporary home there. But Armourer was not a man to be baffled in his evil designs, so taking from his pocket an instrument for picking locks, justice of the peace though

he was, he forced the lock, entered the house, and
searched from room to room, until he found the
chamber in which Joseph Coale was confined by
illness. He took him by the arm, dragged him
downstairs, asked if he would take the Oath of
Allegiance, and on his refusal sent him to the House
of Correction. Thus "this honest man," as Gough
records, " was kept in prison until his death, which
occurred some six years later, in 1670."

" *He who goeth out of the power of God loseth his
liberty,*" writes George Fox.

"Stone walls do not a prison make "

to one who has been set free by Christ, "saved "—
to use Joseph Coale's own words—" from the great
bondage of sin and corruption." We have but few
details of this six years' captivity, but are not surprised
to meet with the following passage in an epistle to
"The beloved Friends of Devon and Cornwall," many
of whom must have been personally known to him ;
" *Neither prison-walls, nor locks, nor the cruelty of
man can obstruct the issues of the Lord's love nor
the manifestation of His presence which is our joy
and comfort, and carries above all sufferings, and
makes days and hours and years pleasant unto us,
which pass away as a moment, because of the enjoyment of seeing Him with whom a thousand years is
but as one day.*"

Meanwhile his friend Thomas Curtis tells George
Fox in a letter : " Our little children kept the meetings up when we were all in prison, notwithstanding
that wicked justice." Some of these children were
treated with such violence by Armourer that they
became black in the face.

In another letter to the Friends of Devon and
Cornwall, Joseph Coale alludes to the death and darkness into which all " have fallen by reason of trans-

gression against the Lord our Creator, out of which He is now redeeming many by His own power, even all those who do lay hold on and receive *the free gift of His love* held forth in our Lord Jesus Christ, . . . given for salvation unto the very ends of the earth, and unto whom they are to look and be saved from the great bondage of sin and corruption."

Joseph Coale died at the age of thirty-four; and, in the two or three pages allotted to his memory in "Piety Promoted," we read that "being filled with heavenly love and life, he laid down his head in peace and full assurance of everlasting life."

We will now turn our attention to Ambrose Rigge, whom Joseph Coale met—perhaps not for the first time—in the county gaol, at Dorchester. Ambrose Rigge, who was born at Barton, in Westmoreland, was one of those seekers after God to whom George Fox's ministry was a heaven-sent message. He had been wont to read the sacred Scriptures, and there were times in his boyhood when the consideration of his spiritual state weighed heavily on his mind. "Being," he says, "a stranger to Him in whom life was and is, I was still in darkness; . . . and notwithstanding I was not so overcome of gross evils, yet I daily found sin reigning and ruling in me. . . . I often cried unto the Lord but saw no way of deliverance."

He went from one clergyman or minister to another, hoping to gain from their teaching what his soul yearned for. But he found them "physicians of no value," for they failed to direct him to Christ, the only unfailing Healer, though they bade him apply the promises and get faith; yet he says that no plaster could cure him whilst the corruption remained. Seeking further, he met with some books which afforded him a little help, whilst he earnestly besought the Lord that if He had any blessing to bestow on him on earth, He would show him His way of truth ; for he saw that many to whom he had been looking for instruction were as bad, if not worse than himself.

This prayer was answered at the time of George Fox's visit to Westmoreland in 1652. Ambrose Rigge believed and received his teaching, because—to use his own words—he felt that " it was indeed the testimony of the Word of God, which became quick and powerful in me, and sharper than a two-edged sword, to the man of sin which had long ruled in my heart." It is evident that not in mere theory, but in deep heart-felt experience, he was led to see that the answer to the cry, " O wretched man that I am, who shall deliver me ?" is, " I thank God through Jesus Christ our Lord." The following verses of his are lacking in poetical merit, but well portray the fulness of his trust in an all-sufficient Saviour :—

> ". . . For by Law's works cannot mankind
> Be justified with Him,
> Until he come this Christ to find,
> With whom I did begin.
>
> Even Israel's Shepherd and their Rock
> To save them from their sin,
> Who now to ope unto His knock,
> And Him receive within.
> He'll give them power His sons to be,
> His daughters eke also,
> And give them perfect victory
> O'er their infernal foe.
> But first He'll purify their hearts
> By His own precious blood,
> And quench the enemy's fiery darts
> When they come as a flood."*

---

* In a letter to Count Zinzendorf, Peter Bohler says :—" Our way of believing in the Saviour is so easy to Englishmen that they cannot reconcile themselves to it ; if it were a little more artfu they would much sooner find their way into it. Of *faith in Jesus*

"The enemy of God," Ambrose Rigge writes, "makes many believe they are well enough—they are church members, and they themselves yielding their members servants to sin. . . . And all these agree together, and with one mouth say they shall never be free from sin while they be upon earth ; and here he deceiveth thousands and overthrows the true faith which gives victory over the world and the prince of it, and leads into the place of holiness within the vail."

He goes on to show that such as held these views were putting more confidence in the devil's ability to uphold his work in them as long as they lived, than in the power of Christ to "destroy the works of the devil," and so according to their faith would it be unto them. And he frankly tells them that such "pleading is against the One Offering which hath 'perfected for ever them that are sanctified'" (Heb. x. 14). In reference to the promise, "If the Son, therefore, shall make you free, ye shall be free indeed," he remarks, that this freedom is obtained by none but those who are *given up* to follow Him.

Perhaps few of the early Friends in the first freshness of their allegiance to their Saviour, had more literally to give up all for Christ than Ambrose Rigge. Forsaken by his father and mother, despised by his acquaintance for a time, like the Lord whom he followed, he had not where to lay his head. Nor did the tempter fail to assail him in the season of trial. But he was to prove that though the power of the enemy is mighty, the power of God is almighty. His soul was raised above these sore troubles, and in the midst of them, "The Lord," he says, "spoke comfort-

---

they have no other idea than the generality of people have. *They justify themselves,* and, therefore, they always take it for granted that they believe already, and try to *prove their faith* by their works, and thus so plague and torment themselves that they are at heart very miserable."

ably with me, and said, ' Fear not, I will be with thee and care for thee. . . . The Good Shepherd drew me in again with his crook, and made me lie down among the sheep of His pasture ; . . . and I became strong in spirit and *in the faith of the Son of God*, by which I obtained victory and freedom over that which long had victory over me."

Thus cast out by his family and friends, and even in the midst of strong temptation, Ambrose Rigge found that the Lord gave him " more and more of His good Spirit," and enabled him to resolve to be His faithful follower at any cost.   He felt a strong inclination to go to London, and obtain some employment amongst the Friends there, but abstained from taking this step because of the conviction that it was God's will that he should remain where he was until called forth to labour for Him.   So he waited for a time, and then believed that he was commissioned to go to the south of England, there to be a witness for Christ, and to suffer many things for Him.   And at first this seemed hard ; for a while he spoke of it to no one, pondering it in his heart, yet without the least intention of disregarding the call if it were confirmed to his soul.   And when he fully and freely surrendered himself to the service, all that he gave up for Christ's sake was little in comparison with " The joy of the Lord," that was his strength.

Thus early in his Christian pilgrimage did Ambrose Rigge learn that one of the sweetest lessons God can teach His children is to say from the depths of a trusting, restful soul, " Thy will be done ;"—when the love of God is so shed abroad in the heart by the Holy Ghost that the struggle to yield to the Divine will— because we know that it is infinitely wise, and that it is a duty thus to yield—ceases ; and the power is given to love that will because it is so absolutely worthy to be loved ;—when the bride thinks less of her possession of the Beloved, and more of being possessed by Him, and finds that the bliss of saying, " I am my Beloved's, and His desire is towards me," coincides with a surrender to Him that has no condition and no reserve.

> " He cannot will me aught but good,
> I trust Him utterly."

Ambrose Rigge tells us that a fellow-traveller was "prepared" for him, a friend named Thomas Robertson, " who was made willing to leave his dear wife and tender babes, to go into the Lord's harvest." It was in the spring of 1665, when Ambrose Rigge was about the age of twenty-one, that after a toilsome journey performed on foot they at length reached London. After passing through various perils, and foreseeing "eminent dangers" in their onward path, can we wonder that they were tempted to return to the North? But the God in whom they trusted could not forsake them, and in His name and power they pursued their journey.

At Dover many were turned from the power of Satan unto God, much of whose blessing manifestly rested on their labours in other Kentish towns and villages. Then " the harvest grew so great, and the labourers being few," they separated from one another in order to pass on more promptly to the western counties, to " proclaim the acceptable day of the Lord " " in cities, towns, and villages."

Ambrose Rigge does not dwell on the self-denial involved in depriving themselves of the solace of companionship, but remarks that as they were strangers and pilgrims upon earth, and had none to direct them but the Lord alone, they were driven to many straits outwardly. But they knew WHOM they had believed; His word of promise could not fail as they trusted in Him, and whatever they had to undergo, courage and strength were given them according to their need.

May we not believe that, truly trusting in their Saviour and leaning on His strength, they knew something of the blessedness of that state in which the command to do or to suffer for Him, and the ready acquiescence to that command, seem to flow simultaneously from the same source ? Yet there is something almost pathetic in the fact, that in Ambrose Rigge's extremely meagre account of their labours, he thinks it worth while to record that once when stopping at a cottage by the wayside for a little water to quench his thirst, the woman who handed it to him told him of a traveller who had called there two or three days before, and who was, he felt sure, no other than his beloved fellow-labourer.

At Chichester, after speaking in a meeting of the Baptists, he was brought before the mayor ; and a justice of the peace was sent for, who threatened to commit him to the *Gate-house.* When his bodily strength was well-nigh spent he drew near Bristol, and soon rallied from the joy of meeting with some Friends, and the refreshment of a brief rest. But he was "pressed in spirit" to go forward, and when visiting two Friends from the north of England, who were imprisoned at Exeter, he once more met with Thomas Robertson, and they resumed their labours together. At Basingstoke, where they had appointed a meeting, they were arrested before its commencement, and tendered the oath of abjuration. Because they could not take it they were committed to prison, and deprived alike of their money, linen, and ink-horns.

It was at first arranged that they should not be allowed the mutual comfort of companionship, but as there were not *two* cells " bad enough " for them, they were " thrust together into a low strait room," while orders were given that any Friends who ventured to visit them should be fined. The windows of their cell were boarded up, and the gaoler refused them the use of candle or fire ; " All which," Ambrose Rigge writes, " we with patience bore till they were weary with their cruelty, by which [endurance] several, both in town and country, were convinced of the Truth." This imprisonment was of nearly three months' duration.

When set at liberty Ambrose Rigge laboured in the Isle of Wight, and also in Hampshire, where, as he went from town to town and village to village, the Lord made his words an effectual message, and many were turned to righteousness.

In Sussex, also, he tells us, " many received the word of God with joy, and met often together ; in whose meetings God manifested His presence and power in large measure." After going back to Hampshire, " to water the tender plants there," he went into Dorsetshire. His treatment in Dorchester gaol, where he met with Joseph Coale, has already been narrated.

On Ambrose Rigge's next visit to Southampton, where his heart was cheered by communion with those amongst whom he had formerly laboured, he thought it right to go to a church where an Independent minister was preaching, and to desire, at the conclusion of the sermon, that he might speak a few words in the fear of God. But the violent treatment he encountered from the congregation almost forbade this. Meanwhile the minister went out, and applied to the magistrates, who caused Ambrose Rigge to be again made a close prisoner. By their orders also a soldier, who had received leave from his commanding officer to call on Ambrose Rigge, was laid hands on at the inn ; his visit was prohibited and his arms taken from him, which treatment he bore in a truly Christian spirit.

When once more at liberty Ambrose Rigge was

constrained by the love of Christ to go to the Isle of Wight. He had planned to sail from Portsmouth, but was prevented by the governor; he then set sail from Hurst Castle, but some Baptists with whom he had conferred betrayed him to " the muster Master," who caused the captain of the vessel to set him on shore again. That night he walked back through the Forest, in heavy rain, to Lymington, where he procured a passage in a boat which was laden with faggots. At Newport, he says, the professors of religion were " rich and full, and rejected the counsel of God, and despised His messenger, sent to them in tender love." Some soldiers soon arrested him, and he was sent out of the island by order of the governor.

But God gave him the power to endure ; and as he still believed that there was a work for him to accomplish in the Isle of Wight, he suffered but little time to elapse before going there again and pursuing his faithful labours amid many hardships. When confined in a prison, described as " cold and filthy," and which stood in the middle of a street, he had good service for his Lord. Doubtless this must have been by preaching to or conversing with the passers by ; for as soon as his intercourse with them was observed he was removed to another prison, and placed in a back room which had no view of the street. " Yet at length the Lord delivered me, he writes, " and there was a meeting settled."

It was about this time that an Act in reference to idle vagrants was often cruelly taken advantage of for the persecution of Friends who were travelling for the furtherance of their religious service. And when next at Southampton Ambrose Rigge was arrested, and, with much abuse, thrown headlong into the " cage."

Nor was this punishment deemed sufficient. The Mayor granted a warrant for his being whipped at the market-place, and after this sentence had been executed by the hangman, Ambrose Rigge was laid across a hand-barrow, and carried through the streets by two men. He was then placed in a cart, and drawn out of the town in frost and snow. No refreshment was given him, and he was told that if he ever revisited the town he should be whipped a second time, and also branded in the shoulder with the letter R.

Soon afterwards, however, he was, as he says, "moved of the Lord" to go to Southampton again; and this time suffered from no molestation, although he held several meetings. But on a subsequent visit the Mayor again threatened him with the utmost rigour of the law, but was prevented by a justice of the peace from carring out his design.

In 1660 Ambrose Rigge underwent a suffering imprisonment at Winchester, because of his conscientious refusal to take the Oath of Allegiance; and two years later he was, for the same reason, committed close prisoner to Horsham gaol, where he was confined for ten years, and was often sorely abused by cruel gaolers. "I was freely resigned," he writes, "to suffer all the days of my life, if it was the will of the Lord, seeing no way of deliverance from man, in whom I put no confidence; but with a godly confidence was resolved to wait in patience all the days of my appointed time."

It was during this imprisonment that Ambrose Rigge married Mary Luxford, the daughter of a certain Captain Luxford, of Hurstpierpoint, who had become a Friend. Mary Rigge's husband writes of her as "a blessed woman." About a year after his release they went to reside at Gatton, where Ambrose Rigge opened a boarding-school, finding time, however, for much good service in the neighbourhood. "Many," he says, "were gathered to the Lord, and established in the faith of the Gospel." It was during his residence at this place that Ambrose Rigge

addressed an Epistle of Advice to Friends, in which
he writes how his spirit had been grieved by "the
uneven walking of many."

He died at Reigate, in 1704, leaving behind him
many seals to his ministry. "I am going," he said,
"where the weary are at rest!"

Thus, in the face of difficulties the magnitude of
which it is hard for us to estimate, did our forefathers
in the faith labour for the advancement of the
Redeemer's kingdom. Nor surely in these days is
there less need of men that have "understanding of
the times to know what Israel ought to do."

And yet of the least in His kingdom the Lord of
Hosts has need to aid in displaying His banner, and
the battle is no sham fight. But Christ has told His
disciples that He will give them "power . . . over all
the power of the enemy." By His "promised"
mercy, by His "Holy Covenant"—nay, by His oath,
—God binds Himself to deliver His believing people
that they may "serve Him without fear in holiness
and righteousness." Distrust of God's grace is not
humility. Even distrust of any gift that He has
bestowed upon us may be the result of an undue
shrinking from responsibility. Therefore, however weak
we are, let us never fear to pray that "all the good
pleasure of His goodness, and the work of faith with
power," may be fulfilled in us. Many and varied are
the kinds of service to which we are called, that none
need fail to make some use, under God's guidance, of
"the wonderful power"—as it has been termed—
"with which He has endowed us, as social and sym-
pathetic beings, to impart what we know and love, to
pass on from hand to hand the torch we bear, be it of
a blazing brightness, or as yet but dimly burning.
But, first of all, we must ourselves possess the light."

V.

THOMAS GWIN—MERCHANT AND MINISTER.

"It is said of God's people that they had an eye unto Him and were enlightened, and their faces were not ashamed. So now Jesus *undertakes for thee and for thy faith.* He saith, I will be an enemy to thy enemies, and an adversary to thy adversaries.

"God the Father is looking on; angels are beholding; all heaven is interested. Nay, had'st thou but eyes to see, thou wouldst behold — like the prophet's servant — mountains around thee full of horses, and chariots of fire, all engaged for thy defence. Shout, then, for the victory is already obtained by Jesus for His people. . . Thanks be to God who giveth us the victory, through our Lord Jesus Christ."

HAWKER.

THOMAS GWIN—MERCHANT AND MINISTER.

———◆◆◆———

> " Here finds my heart its rest,
>   Response that knows no shock,
> The strength of love that keeps it blest
>   In THEE, the riven Rock:
> My soul as girt around
> Her citadel hath found :
> I would love Thee as Thou lovest me
>   O Jesus most desired."—*From the Latin.*

WE glean some interesting particulars concerning "Thomas Gwin, merchant, late of Falmouth, and thrice mayor of said town," from an old MS. quarto volume, of 646 closely-written pages, copied from the somewhat mutilated original journal. In his " Will and Testament" he writes :—

" Some may be apt to say, Here is good moral doctrine, but nothing relating to faith in our Lord Jesus Christ. I must, indeed, acknowledge that without faith it is impossible to please Him. But some men, whether drawn to it by heat of dispute or by their own critical disposition, have made systems of faith (and tied people to them under penalty of damna-- tion) that can scarcely be understood by one in his senses. Such systems are wrongfully called ' Articles of Faith ; ' it is another sort from that of the Apostle, ' If thou shalt con- fess with thy mouth the Lord Jesus, and shalt believe in thine heart that God raised Him from the dead, thou shalt be saved.' . . . Dearest Father, into Thy hands I commit and commend my spirit, not trusting in any merits of mine own, for I have merited nothing of myself, but on Thy abundant love and mercy in Thy blessed Son our Lord, I place my whole confidence and trust, now and for ever. Amen.

Thomas Gwin was born at Falmouth, in the spring of 1656, and was brought up by respectable parents, who sent him when eight years old to a grammar school, where his education was carried on during the five following years. His mind, he says, "was busy and inquisitive" about religion; he saw how little a form of godliness would avail without the power, and sometimes when alone would earnestly seek for pardon from God.

At the age of fourteen he was sent to France for the sake of acquiring the language, and found it "somewhat tedious to part from his tender parents." He was much exposed to evil companionship at Rochelle, and in later life thankfully believed that a severe illness had to some extent preserved him from this danger. His great weakness, and the wickedness by which he was surrounded, made him so anxious to return home, that in 1671, in the depth of winter, he embarked in a very small vessel. For nearly four weeks she was tossed about at sea, often in great peril whilst those on board were unsupplied with fresh water, bread, or candles. "One of the worst and most dangerous of passages," Thomas Gwin calls it, and earnest were his desires that if God spared his life he might ever be thankful to Him.

Joyful as was his reception at home he found ere long that storms of another kind were near at hand. Soon after his return his mind was much impressed by John i. 9, in which Christ is called "The true Light which lighteth every man that cometh into the world." This text was quoted in his presence by someone who was giving an account of a discussion between a clergyman and a Friend; and in connection with other portions of Scripture it convinced Thomas Gwin, he says, that it was his "duty to leave the formal worships of the world and joyne myselfe with the despised people called Quakers." What he most dreaded in pursuing this course was the displeasure of his father. For a while he accompanied him to church, although distressed by the belief that it was no longer right to do so.   But one day feeling that he could not thus continue to disregard the leading of the heavenly Shepherd, he quietly quitted his parent's side and turned back ; this circumstance of course led to inquiry, and he frankly avowed his views.   His father's anger was great, and he manifested his displeasure for nearly two years.

The loss of his father's love was to Thomas Gwin like the loss of life itself, though the God of all comfort did not fail him.   On one occasion, when the elder Gwin's anger was more violent than usual, his son's mind was kept in great calmness, " And it opened in me," he writes, " that I should stand still and see God's salvation, for the enemyes I then saw I should thenceforth see no more for ever ; and I do not remember that ever after that time he was so outrageous again."

Thomas Gwin now spent much time in reading the Scriptures, thinking his pocket unfurnished if it did not contain a Bible ; and often as his eye fell on a text his heart at once melted within him.   He especially delighted in Isaiah's prophecies concerning the Redeemer, wounded for his transgressions and bruised for his iniquities.   He was diligent in his attendance of meetings.   " Many sweet openings," he writes, " I was acquainted with, and some ravishments of sense in devotion, the Lord feeding of mee and caring for mee though a child."

When about the age of eighteen he believed that God was calling him to the ministry of the Gospel, which he says was a hard exercise because of his bashfulness.   His anxiety clearly to discern his duty towards God and man was great ; and the Lord was his strength in the time of need.   His offerings in the ministry were, however, almost discontinued for several years, partly in consequence of a public expression of disapproval from " an antient Friend " who was present at a meeting in which Thomas Gwin had spoken briefly. "I was somewhat willing," the latter humbly says, "to judge myselfe rather than him mistaken in judgment."

Thomas Gwin sometimes acted as companion to Friends who were on ministerial journeys, and to one of these especially, Richard Samble, of Falmouth, he became much attached. "Our dear friend, brother and neighbour," he styles him, when recording his death in 1680, "who had been made as a cloude full of rain to drop down upon the tender seed here and elsewhere." Brought up a member of the Church of England, Richard Samble had earnestly sought the Lord in his early youth, and about the age of twenty-two experimentally learnt the way of salvation when Cornwall, his native county, was visited by some Friends. One of his contemporaries says that he "waited on the Lord for wisdom, till his heart was filled with the power of the Lord like a vessel with new wine." When at home he worked industriously at his trade, which was that of a tailor, but he travelled much in England and Wales.

When on one of these missions Richard Samble was taken ill in Dorsetshire. To his Cornish friends he wrote : "The Lord hath been pleased to make this sick bed unto me better than a king's palace. I do rejoice in the Lord, who doth so sweetly visit me with the glorious light of His countenance. It is with me as with one who has travelled many weary journeys, and at last hath come to the sight of his desired end." Regaining a little strength he attempted to return home, but could get no further than Clampet, in Devonshire, where he was joined by his wife. "Oh! my dear wife, come hither to me," he said, "and let me take thee in my arms once more. The Lord will be to thee a husband, and a father to our little children as thou abidest faithful to Him." As long as life lasted, we are told, he was praising and magnifying the Lord.

One of his friends writes of "all things being sanctified to him in the fear of the Lord," and of his willingness to serve God "with all his heart, mind, understanding and strength." He died at the age of thirty-six.

Thomas Gwin, although engaged in his father's shop, regularly attended the meetings of Friends, including those held monthly and quarterly; and whilst his hope and prayer was that the Lord would accomplish His work in his soul, he learnt that "It's sure we must walk by faith and not by sight." After a time his father treated him with much kindness, whilst keeping him as much as possible under his authority.

In 1685 Thomas Gwin was the only Cornish Friend who went to London to attend the Yearly Meeting, and he at first felt it a very formidable affair to give an account of the condition of the meetings in his native county; but he soon found that the Lord gave him the needed wisdom. He now became acquainted with "some antient and honourable Friends," including George Fox and Stephen Crisp. His homeward journey was an adventurous one, on account of the conflict between the King and the Duke of Monmouth; for the Lord Mayor had declined giving him a pass because he was a Dissenter. Soon after his return to Falmouth he was brought low by illness, and in bodily weakness learnt more fully not to trust in himself, but in that Saviour who healeth the wounds of His people. It was about this time that the hearts of the Cornish Friends were gladdened by a visit from Leonard Fell and Roger Haydock, for the severe persecution of that period prevented ministers from often visiting the far west.

Early in 1687 Thomas Gwin married Elizabeth Whitford, of Liskeard, who was sixteen years of age. Thomas Lower was very desirous that this union should take place; and when he saw Thomas

Gwin at a Quarterly Meeting at Tregongeeves, he took him into his chamber in order to converse with him on the subject, and then conducted him to the home of Thomas Salthouse, where the young lady and her mother were lodging. The latter, Thomas Gwin tells us, " did give allowance that I might visit her daughter." The marriage was a happy one.

The first great trial which befell the young parents was the death of their little son, of fifteen months old. " A very hopeful child," his father calls him ; " but in the will of God," he adds, " we were made content, and bore it with patience, and our love abounded to each other, in the fear of God, when we were thus made joynt sufferers." A few months later the death of Thomas Gwin's father occurred ; and a little son who was born about that time only lived for ten weeks. In the summer of 1690, however, the birth of a daughter, who was named after her mother, seemed to make amends for their former losses. Her father says : " We nursed her up with care, and she lay in our bosoms. Whether we were thankful enough or not for soe great mercy I know not, but after twenty months the Lord took her away."

Not long afterwards, when writing to congratulate his friend William Ellis on the birth of a son, he says : " As for my part, I have been exceedingly exercised by the removing of my little daughter ; . . . but it has been the Lord's will since then to give me another, who I desire may grow up in God's fear ; for I have a true unity with thee in thy concern on account of Friend's children. . . . The Lord, I beseech Him, turn away this careless and lukewarm spirit, and engage the young generation in zeal and fervency in His service." It was just at this time that Thomas Gwin wrote " A little Epistle to Friends' Children and Young Folkes."

The persecution of Friends had now for some time

abated, and Thomas Gwin writes of speaking in meetings on "watchfulness against indifference and lukewarmness, which, in these days of ease, too easily prevayled on many." In 1692 Thomas Gwin's heart was gladdened by the birth of his daughter Anne, who, surviving a very delicate childhood, became a great comfort to her parents, as did her sister Grace, who was born two years later.

Thomas Gwin suffered frequently and severely from attacks of gout, but writes of being "well content therein," because of the "sweet refreshments and the love of God, which made the payne the more tolerable;" and he would tell his visitors of the Lord's wonderful dealings, and press them to seek after Him. When he was thus laid aside from active life, one of the two week-day meetings held at Falmouth often took place in his chamber. Once or twice, also, when thus confined by illness, the children's weekly meeting —of which he seems to have had the chief, or entire, charge—was held at his house. He often visited the meetings of Friends in his own county, and we find many allusions in his diary to meetings held in neighbouring villages, which were sometimes largely attended by the public.

When writing of his "tender regard for the fellowship of brethren," and of the need of waiting on God for the renewal of strength, Thomas Gwin says :— " I knew noe place strong enough for safety besides the name of the Lord. In His power I was strengthened, in whose presence is life, and at whose right hand there are pleasures for evermore." The following brief entry in Thomas Gwin's diary, early in 1703, seems too suggestive in its quaint simplicity to be passed by :—

" John Ellis came to visit me, to whom I spoke sharply and earnestly as to his neglect of their Monthly Meeting, &c. *Quære*—Whether I was too much transported with zeal, and whether, if I had waited and spoken out of the haste, it might not have been more benefitt to him, and more comfort to myselfe, although his behaviour to the meeting seemed rude and not orderly ? "

A week or two later he writes of speaking in meeting on the need of God's people being willing in the day of His power, and the necessity of waiting for this power ; and a renewed sense of God's love was graciously granted to himself and to the meeting. At a Quarterly Meeting not long afterwards we find him alluding " to the gifts and abilities of some men, how capable they might be to serve Truth if their minds were not in the world." When describing a parting interview with some of his friends, at the time of another Quarterly Meeting, he adds, " My mouth was opened as to the excellency of those seasons, but that we might not rest on them, but might draw near to Jesus, who would abide with us."

Thomas Gwin attended the Yearly Meeting of 1704. He records how John Gratton spoke at "Grace Street" (Gracechurch Street), concerning "those who believe in Christ obtaining eternall life," with earnest persuasions to his hearers ; and of how at Devonshire House James Dickenson dwelt on the glory and beauty of Truth, and John Gratton on poverty of spirit ; the latter relating an anecdote of his countrywoman, Joan of Darby, who *could* suffer, but *could not* dispute.

" We had sundry sweet seasons of God's love. . . . In the Meeting of Ministering Friends, John Fothergill spoke concerning leaders causing the people to err, &c.; rebuked by George Whitehead, who spoke of the benefit of love.

" After me stood up a young man of the North, pretty zealous and fervent, but pretty long considering John Gratton and Thomas Upthaw were there, who were both very sweetly engaged as usual. . . . On the 6th, J. Gratton spoke ; a proclamation of love with which his heart was filled, ' There is a river the streams whereof shall make glad the city of God ;' how sweetly the Lord caused it to flow (I could hardly for-

bear crying out, Oh, yes! all that are athirst, let them come!),
cautions against damming up the river by disobedience, &c.
He was greatly enlarged about the 'flowing streams of God's
love.' At another meeting John Gratton spoke on Christ's
command—'Feed my sheep.'"

As was his usual practice, Thomas Gwin visited
many meetings on his homeward way. Soon after his
return we find him at Marazion, exhorting "Friends
and people against settling down in a forme of godly-
nesse—the great advantage of those that *come to the
power which was near to people if they could believe
in it, to help them against the enemy's power*, so that
nothing should be able to harm them." At Kea
meeting, a week or two later, he spoke of the woman
who was healed by touching the hem of Christ's garment, and urged his hearers to come likewise to Jesus
that they might be cured of the disease of sin. "I
find," he writes, in allusion to his ministry, that "the
fellowship of the Spirit is become strength, life, courage
and faith, and makes up all my wants who am often
very poor."

In an early entry in his diary for 1705, Thomas
Gwin refers to a week-day meeting which was a "fresh
season, more than can soon be expressed," during
which he spoke of his conviction that "what hindered
good meetings was *the coming to them without faith
and fervency of spirit.*"

Of the next Yearly Meeting Thomas Gwin remarks,
that "on the whole, the Meeting was pretty peaceable
and ended soe." Yet it seems that this tranquillity
had been somewhat endangered by a Friend who
brought in "certain queryes." Thomas Gwin says,
that to him this occasion did not seem to be attended
with "soe sweet a channel of life as sometimes;" but
wisely adds, that perhaps his feelings were influenced
by the fact that he was "low and weak in himselfe."
On his return journey he was present at a Quarterly

Meeting at Taunton, where he thought it right to speak
in the meeting, of "how serviceable some might be in
the Church did they but serve Truth as readily as they
did the world." At Okehampton, where he spent a
First-day, he was "exceedingly drawne forth to those
that came in, ... and abundantly exercised to
declare ye day of God's visitation to them."

But we must not in the minister wholly forget the
merchant. Soon after his return to Falmouth, whilst
tried with bodily suffering and nervous depression, he
meets with "extraordinary trouble and abundance of
disappointment" with respect to the purchase of pilchards. "The Lord knows," he says, "it was a time
of much exercise and temptation to mee, and soe I
note it. The Lord sanctify all and bring it to an happy
end." Yet in the midst of this trial he finds joy in
helping to bring to a satisfactory termination a dispute
about some unsettled accounts between two Friends at
Penryn. Not long afterwards we read of meetings at
Looe, Polperro, and also at St. Keverne, where he spoke
of the tidings of great joy at the birth of Christ, as the
best tidings that ever came to the sons and daughters
of men.

In the spring of 1706, Thomas Gwin took his eldest
daughter to Bath, visiting many meetings on his
journey thither. After a reference to that at Glaston-
bury, he writes :—"1 rid to see our friend John Banks
who told me he had a weak vessell but good treasure in
it. We conferred for more than an houre, and I was
comforted in the company of so antient a father."*
After leaving his daughter at Bath, Thomas Gwin
spent a day or two at Bristol, and alludes to a meeting
there as being "a sweet season of love and living
openesse towards the mourners in Zion." He elsewhere
writes :—

---

* For Sketch of John Banks, see *Friends' Examiner*, No. XXV.,
1873.

" Did poor souls but see how much the Lord loves them,
even in this dejected condition, and how He is hereby teaching them humility and exalting the blessed government of the
Lord Jesus Christ, they would hope more and fear less, and say
with one of old, ' It's the Lord ; let Him do whatever He
sees fit.' "

A General Meeting for Devon and Cornwall was
held this year, which lasted four hours, ending at 6 p.m.
Thomas Gwin describes it as a season of refreshment
and sweet flowing of love. It took place on the day
after a Quarterly Meeting. Some Ministers from a
distance were present. In reading Thomas Gwin's
diary, one is surprised at the considerable number of
visits paid to Cornwall by Friends engaged in the
work of the ministry. The names of several of these
good men and women are quite unfamiliar, and not to
be found in the early literature of our Society.

Thomas Gwin's sermons were often long, probably
undesirably so, sometimes occupying an hour, an hour
and half, or even more. But his heart was very full of his
message.   He thus writes of a meeting at Penryn :—

" Tho' feeling very empty I stood up in a little faith given
but oh ! the great openesse and enlargement brought on my
spirit.   I had matter in abundance, and it flowed as a spring,
and though I shortened my words, having regard to the
people who stood long, yet was my spirit filled with love and
my mouth with expression, and when I ceased preaching, I
kneeled downe in the same lively sence which still continued or
increased upon mee, so that I could render praises and thanks-
giving to God, through Jesus Christ our Lord, and beg His blessing on the opportunity, and in His peace and love we parted."

In the latter part of this year Thomas Gwin suffered
from a long and dangerous illness, when violent pain
was at times his portion ; " Yet," he says, " was my
spirit easy, blessed be the Lord, so that looking to Him
and His goodness, it frequently made me say, What
manner of love is this !" Thus from his own experience

he could speak not long afterwards in meeting, of
" the state of a languishing body being better than
that of a languishing mind." About this time, when
writing of a mid-week meeting, he says that he had
a season of sweet counsel to the effect that " our
meetings should not be counted slight matters or of so
little consequence as some may imagine ; if we attend
them aright they may be seasons of meeting with the
Lord, and by this means we wax stronger."

In the summer of 1707 one of his little daughters
was taken ill with what was supposed to be a slight
attack of small-pox. At the same time Thomas Gwin
was suffering from a severe attack of gout, yet writes
of the Lord's goodness making him " sweetly content
under bitter pains." But the next entry in his diary
is a very sorrowful one.

" I was still at home with the gout, but then came a
tempestuous sea of afflictions, one billow beating after
another, which might prove of great danger; but blessed be
the Lord whose hand sustained me under all, and enabled
me in the midst of heart-piercing trouble to bless His Holy
Name. My brother, Daniel Gwin, who had been hurt by a
fall (but we hoped not dangerously), waxed very ill and dyed
the next morning. Whilst I went to visit him, my sweet
Jenny sickened again, and fell into a violent fever, which
increased upon her, notwithstanding doctor's advice and all
our cares and endeavours, so that in two days and a halfe she
dyed, about one in the morning, after some pretty expressions, and was sensible to her last minutes, leaving abundance
of grief on our spirits (only in the will of God was our peace
and rest), and was then not a full day more than 4½ years
old. My brother was buryed the 28th, and my child the
30th. Thomas Giddy preached at our meeting-house, and
I was made to praise God at conclusion in the midst of my
great sadness. Many people accompanied us to her funeral,
and there was a great auditory at the meeting-house. In her
sickness I could not beg her life, but in my approaches to
the Lord must leave her to His will. Amen. Her saying
when near her end that she was to have a golden bed was
memorable ; her care to have some toys paid for, and sundry

expressions in her health, showed her honesty and fear of evil-doing. The Lord was very good to me in comforting me in my tribulations, and though I had not any words at meetings the week following, yet was my soul blessed with a sense of His good which is beyond all temporall enjoyments."

So with the poet he might have said :—

> " Oh, blessed Life—the heart at rest
> When all without tumultuous seems
> That trusts a higher will and deems
> That higher will, not mine, the best."

A few days after little Jenny's funeral, her sister Margery became ill of small-pox, and her parents feared lest they should lose her also. Yet of this time of deep trial Thomas Gwin could still say that "the Lord took out much of the sting." But his little girl soon began to recover.

In allusion to a Monthly Meeting held about this time, Thomas Gwin tells us that in the men's meeting he spoke "touching the zeal and strength attending our Friends in their coming forth at first, obtained by having their spirits exercised in God's law. The like exercise would now produce like effects." Again he writes :—"The sense of the Lord's goodness dwelling in my spirit made me glad in meetings, and left me not on my return from them. . . . The renewed sense of God's love sometimes dropped on me as rain." And he refers to a memorable season in meeting, when he thought it right to invite his friends " to taste and see how good the Lord is, that He is best to His people when they have most need of Him ! "

Now that the persecution of Friends had almost ceased, great was Thomas Gwin's desire that they should keep on their "inward armour in the day of outward ease." In one of his epistles he says :—

" Was the adversary busy among our elder brethren, to distress and persecute them, and think you that he is now fallen asleep or less busy in his endeavours than in former days ?　No, surely ; he cares not what thy profession may be, if he can estrange thee from the life of Jesus, from a fellowship with Him. . . . May the same ancient zeal and love of God abound amongst us that did among our elder brethren, who loved not their lives, liberties, or estates, so as to be kept thereby from their duty, and from seeking and serving the Lord with fervency of spirit."

Thomas Gwin was very frequently engaged in visiting meetings in his own neighbourhood, to which apparently the public were often invited.　Nor did he forget to call on the aged, infirm, and afflicted.　An early entry in his diary for 1708, records a visit to "an antient, poor Friend, Ursula Stephens, then sick in bed," who was greatly comforted by his counsel and prayer.　He also remembered those who were in prison.

At a Monthly Meeting which took place soon afterwards, Thomas Gwin was sent for by his wife "to help her against some fiery contentious spirits that had with violence fallen upon her at the Women's Meeting, whom all the Friends there could not keep in temper ; but all tended to hurry and confusion. However," adds Thomas Gwin, "I was kept very quiet and still in my mind, after a little commotion at first hearing them, and it was nothing to me."

At the next Yearly Meeting Thomas Gwin was nominated as one of the clerks, but did not accept the appointment ; he attended all the select committees for drawing up the Epistle, "The addresse to the Queen," &c.　He also alludes to a visit to William Penn, "in the place of his confinement, who was very kind, and told mee, noe man loved mee better than he. . . . Some days before, on meeting William Meade, he very kindly saluted mee, and offered mee one of G. Ff's doctrinall books, which I kindly accepted."

One of the towns visited by Thomas Gwin when

returning to the West, was Street, where, in company
with other friends, he again called on his "antient
friend John Banks," and the interview was one of
mutual comfort.   One day in the summer of this year
Thomas Gwin rode to the Land's End to attend the
funeral of a lady, probably a Friend, who had resided
at Penzance.   Standing on a tomb he spoke for more
than an hour to an assembly consisting, it was supposed,
of three or four hundred people, several of whom
were, he tells us, " of some quality in the world."

About a week later he again went to the Land's
End, this time to be present at a marriage, and thus
describes the event :—" The young man spoke well,
and delivered his marriage vowes ; the maiden could
scarcely be heard.   She was called on to speak louder,
but her words being repeated, she owned them ; after
which I spoke somewhat."   At a meeting soon afterwards we find him

"speaking largely as to who those are the Lord blesses ;
those that are poor, and hungry, and in want, and who come
in faith to lay hold of Jesus Christ.   Others throng about
Him, but draw not virtue from Him.   I spoke of the Lord's
being everywhere the discoverer of the thoughts ; how this
should comfort those that seek after Him, and be a terrour
to evildoers."

The next Quarterly Meeting was a time of trial to
Thomas Gwin, for his little daughter Margery was
taken very ill on the previous day ; and before the
meeting had ended he was called out of it to his sick
child.   His spirit was refreshed at the parting meeting
the next day.   A meeting had also been appointed for
the evening of that day at the house of John Scan-
tlebury, of Falmouth, but, to his disappointment, the
Friends at whose request it had been arranged did not
arrive ; they tarrying by the way, Thomas Gwin says,
and " entering into some discourses about regulation
of apparell and furniture, which seemed not to have

any extraordinary tendency at that time to promote religion."

Soon, we find Thomas Gwin again laid aside by a long and very suffering illness; during its continuance the Monthly Meetings were sometimes held at his house; his heart was also cheered by "very comfortable" letters from some of his friends, and he was thankful to the Lord for abundantly opening his heart to reply to them. But a greater trial was at hand, for his " dear little Margery" became ill of a violent fever, which proved fatal. " She was a sweet, comfortable companion," her father says, " but I was made to give her up to the will of God, and I dared not strive against Him, soe though this was a very sorrowful exercise, yet we sorrowed not as those that have no hope." Just at this time, and whilst his physical suffering was often extreme, he could yet take a lively interest in " sundry accounts of the good meeting Friends had at London," and derive happiness from the reception of a letter. "I had a very comfortable epistle," he writes, " from my antient friend, George Knipe, which ministered refreshment to mee; blessed be the name of the Lord, who did, by His divine power, sustain mee, and led mee, and fed mee with heavenly bread."

When he first ventured out again to meeting, he was carried by two porters in a chair, and although unable to rise from it, he preached for about an hour and-a-half, and prayed at the conclusion of the meeting. A few days later, when the week-day meeting was held at his house, he says that he " spoke forth several things that were as the mysteryes of the kingdom, particularly that *we may know the Lord to do all in us.*" And a week or two later he writes, " I satt and spoke that when God's people gathered *in earnest cry and diligent inquiry* after Him, then their sacrifice came up as incense, and the lifting up of their hands was acceptable to Him." Again he says, " I spoke

pretty much on how the love of God would engage us
where it dwelt in the soule, to meet together oftener
than on First-days."

When he had regained a little strength he one day
attended a meeting at Kea, which had been appointed
by John Fothergill and Gilbert Thomson, who were
visiting Cornwall. He returned home very weary, but
was called up in the night, and told of the arrival of a
boat from Gerrans with a messenger, who came to
inform him of the alarming illness of his brother
Michael, who was anxious to see him; but on his
arrival Thomas Gwin found him at the point of expir-
ing. "This was a very sorrowful season," writes
Thomas Gwin, "when the wound of my little Margery's
departure was scarcely healed."

Towards the end of the year he writes :—

"Henry Atkinson was with us again, whose service was
the less for the tone that attended him; but there was with
him Thomas Chalkley, of Philadelphia, an approved minister,
who spoke very sweetly and invitingly to all. He spoke of
the Lord being a fountain; of the fruits of the Spirit; of
Achsah, who, when she enjoyed the south land was not
content without the upper and nether springs. The south
land he compared to blessings of this life, the springs to
divine comforts. He spoke against *over-caring*, in the
instances of the plowman and merchant, whose affairs
prospered not the more for their excessive care, &c. . . . It
was a blessed thing *to know our relation to the Lord;* most
there had a knowledge by the hearing of the ear, but those
came to peace who became acquainted with Him; the benefitt
of living with Him and abiding in His Tabernacle. Men and
women were false many times in their love, but our blessed
Lord was Truth itselfe, a never-failing help, against whom
the gates of hell should never prevail. We might all know
more of Him. It was a comfortable season of refreshment."

In reference to a week-day meeting not long afterwards, Thomas Gwin writes, "After long silence I
said God had lengthened out time to some of us that
we might tell the younger, and all those that fear

the Lord, what He hath done for our soules." Early
in 1710, when recovering from one of his suffering
attacks of illness, we find Thomas Gwin paying a
visit to the small meeting at the Land's End, this
time accompanied by Kate Reall, a Friend who resided
at Falmouth. In the evening they had a large
meeting at Penzance, when we learn, "abundance
of fine people came in and were extraordinary sober,"
to whom Thomas Gwin says he was "exceedingly
opened and enlarged. Next day I returned home
with Kate Reall; I had been greatly helped in my
service, yet was weak of myselfe, and a very nothing
without Divine help." In allusion to another meeting
he says: "I had a concerne to call with, 'Ho, every
one that is athirst, come ye to the waters'; that *God's
love was so free that we had need only to be thirsty to
partake of it.*" When again ill, he addressed some
friends who called on him, on the blessedness of
becoming "familiarly acquainted" with the Lord.
And when again able to attend meetings he says :—

"I spoke largely as to people's praying that God's kingdom
might come, that I doubted many did it as birds who are
taught to speak, not knowing the meaning of what they say.
I did earnestly and openly set forth the benefitts of that
kingdom, and the advantages of those that were subject to
Him, His care over them and love to them."

Concerning a Monthly Meeting Thomas Gwin writes
that things went well until he proposed that it should
be made a rule that whoever laid out money on behalf
of the meeting should bring an account to the next
Monthly Meeting.

"On which," he says, "E. B., supposing I had reflected on
account brought in by him, stormed greatly, saying I made
it my businesse through prejudice, to reflect on him and his
family as well in my public preaching as then. It pleased
the Lord to keep mee in great quietnesse, blessed be His
name, and I committed the case to the Lord whom I desired

to be judge betwixt us, as knowing that my preaching and speeches have been not in ill-will to any, but in the love of the Truth that they may be saved."

A few days later he records a dream, in which he seemed to be in a meeting " with sundry ancient Friends of the first convincement. A Friend asking them what manner of meetings they had in the beginning, they spoke much of that life, peace and comfort that abounded amongst them. On which E. B. whispered mee (as one affected therewith), ' What accounts doe these Friends give ! Why is it not soe now ? ' On which my mouth was opened, and I said that the peace and comfort was still the same as ever ; to such as truly waited upon God the abounding of it was knowne, but if people came to them heavily and dully, or their minds occupied in other affaires, it was no marvell that those missed the sweet consolation of the Spirit that the diligent and watchful were made partakers of."

Again, and not in a dream, he says : " The cause why people do not enjoy more of the precious life is because they do not find the Lord, the living fountain ; and the cause they do not find Him is, because they do not seek Him with all their hearts." About this time a new meeting-house was built at Kea, and we find Thomas Gwin thus writing of a meeting for transacting the affairs of the Church : " We had a pretty quiet meeting, but great difficulty in raising the money for the house at Kea ; some were close, and some crosse."

At a meeting held at his own house, Thomas Gwin spoke to his friends of the certainty that there is a spring wherewith God refreshes the travellers towards Zion, a well of living waters given to waiting souls. Many, he said, " sit short of it, and though they came to meetings, do not meet this spring. The reason is they do not earnestly seek it, their love being unto other objects." At another time we find him saying, " *Those who partake of the bread of life cannot hold inviting others to come and share with them.*" About this time we find a reference in the diary to Kate Reall's return from London. The certificate sent to Kate Reall during her absence is now before me; it is signed by Thomas Gwin and several other Friends.

"From our Monthly Meeting at Falmᵒ the 8th day of Third Month, 1711. To all our friends whom these may concern. Whereas our friend Katherine Reall did two months ago earnestly importune us to grant her a Certificate, and since her being from home hath again desired yᵉ Same. . . . These are thereon to Certifye yᵗ yᵉ Sᵈ Katherine, since her Return hither from Ireland abᵒ 5 years agoe has been a member of this meeting and hath lived as far as we know a Sober Innocent life no way attended wᵗʰ Reproach, nor any blot on her Conversation, but hath generally behaved herself in her dealings and Convers as a regular Friend ought to Doe."

The " E. B.," to whom allusion has already been made, had a serious attack of illness, falling down senseless in a meeting. Thomas Gwin visited him and prayed at his bedside. Some months later Thomas Gwin spoke in Falmouth Meeting of his desire that those who had been educated in a profession of religion might know it in its living power, and after offering prayer concluded the meeting by the quotation of the text, " Blessed are they that hear the word of God and keep it." " After which," he says, " I was assaulted in my house by E. B. and wife, the woman calling me Fool, &c., all which I bore contentedly and sweetly for the Truth's sake."

In 1712 Thomas Gwin again attended the Yearly Meeting, taking his daughter Anne with him. After giving some account of the meetings visited in the course of their journey, Thomas Gwin writes :—

" The week following we were dayly at the Yearly Meeting,

where we wanted not contests. The first dispute was in relation to entering the sufferings of such as refused to affirm.* Soon after a minute was brought in by some members of the Meeting for Sufferings desiring the Yearly Meeting to explain their minute of 1703, touching the solicitation to be made by those dissatisfied [with the affirmation as it then stood] and whether that was not now accomplished, that the satisfied might then proceed to solicit [Parliament] for its continuance as it now is. There was great debate on this, but at last it was allowed they might solicit next session of Parliament, but in case they succeeded not, then the satisfied were to endeavour to its continuance. But this they would not consent to, nor to a minute drawn up by Thomas Ellwood; but after many days' debate, in which we came to noe end, it was committed to 8 Friends, 4 of each party, viz. :—

George Whitehead		Wm. Penn	
Thos. Ellwood	pro.	Jo. Pike	con.
Ben. Coale		Robert Haydock	
Jo. Wyeth		Roderick Forbes	

who agreed on the following minute, that 'The disatisfied should proceed to solicit next session, and in case they obtained not, noe endeavours should be used to destroy the present affirmation; and the satisfied to concur in such solicitations.' This took, they being wearied with disputes. During all this controversy I said almost nothing of either side, being altogether unwilling to promote faction. I had somewhat in my mind of opposing disputes by showing their nature, but they were so warme of both sides there was little room. . . . Other matters were soon finished, but this dispute made it hold 11 days, that might otherwise end in less than half the time. The parting meeting was not attended with usuall freshnesse."

After leaving London, Thomas Gwin spent a day or two at Reading, where he held a meeting, at the conclusion of which William Penn offered prayer;

---

* It was not until nine years later that an Act of Parliament was passed for accepting the affirmation of Friends in its present form. The one then in use was very unsatisfactory to those who considered that it almost amounted to an oath.

and they had some " loving converse " at the house of
a Friend where Thomas Gwin dined, William Penn
telling him that he ought to have lodged at his house.
Many other meetings were visited by Thomas Gwin on
his return journey, which was a toilsome and painful one
on account of his bodily weakness, and three falls from
his horse.   Yet he often had the pleasure of the companionship of Friends who were on their homeward way.
Soon after his return Falmouth Meeting was visited by
" one William Fawcett, a printer ; who spoke mostly
as to brotherly love, against evill surmises, and a religious selfe that would exercise itselfe in seeing faults
abroad, but could not see any other."

A little later, Thomas Gwin writes of a week of
"little businesse, much pains and leisure," when his
greatest care was the fear that " a ship of Bristoll "
would arrive for a cargo of pilchards long before they
were ready.   As he was able to sit up, one of the two
week-day meetings was held in his chamber.   " To this
meeting," he writes, " came E. B., who upon some
disgusts had abstained from my house two or three
months ; but he seemed kind and I received him
with love. . . . It was a blessed season, and my heart
was enlarged, and my mouth opened near an hour."

Of a similar occasion we find the following account :—" Friends met at my chamber.   Kate Reall
spoke : ' To what end are your sacrifices ? ' and seemed
to bear hard ; soe toward the end I took it up and
said, Whatever was written beforetime, or is now
spoken, I would have none to be discouraged who seek
the Lord in poverty.   Those sentences were intended
for a sinful nation, a people laden with iniquity."

It seems often to have been Thomas Gwin's concern
to urge his hearers to beware of " the great temptations," as he says, " of placing the mind on the earth,
since the heart will be where the treasure is."   Nor
can we wonder at this.   " The spirit of the world is

for ever altering, impalpable ; for ever eluding in fresh forms your attempts to seize it." * Yet in what century has not this spirit of the world eaten as doth a canker into the heart of religion ? Long before the birth of Christ did a prophet say : " All people will walk every one *in the name of his god.*" Have we quite done with idols yet in our Christian England ? In the paths of commerce are none of her sons, in the very vigour of their days, walking in the name of the god Mammon ? Are none of her fair daughters walking in the name of the goddess Fashion ? " For all people *will walk* everyone in the name of his god." But if Jehovah is our God let us say with the same old prophet : " And we will walk in the name of the Lord our God for ever and ever ; " endeavouring to prove practically the reality of our religion to an age characterised alike by much seeking after a just God of love on the one hand, and by much unbelief on the other :—

> " Think not rashly that, because
> Modern life is smooth and fine,
> 'Tis not subject to the laws
> Of the Master's high design :
> That we less require endurance
> Than in days of coarser plan,—
> That we less demand assurance
> Of the Godhead hid in man."

The autumn of this year was a time of severe trial to Thomas Gwin. He had purchased pilchards at St. Ives to the value of £690, at the request of a merchant (apparently of Bristol) who coolly let them lie on his hands. In addition to this, he writes of meeting with " sundry cross accidents and losses ; " whilst he suffered much pain in consequence of a bad fall from his horse. "And what was worse," he sorrowfully adds, " I seemed not so given up to the will of God as I should,

---

* Frederic Robertson.

and a fear lest a discontented, impatient spirit should
enter ; under all which, however, was a secret hand
which sustained." About this time he was comforted
by a visit paid to Falmouth Meeting by Lydia
Lancaster ; and in the midst of his sorrows it would
seem that he was learning advanced lessons of trust in
God ; for we find him praying, " Lord, teach me to live
by faith, that in the greatest trouble and want of sense
(feeling) I may depend on Thy holy arm, and cast my
soul on Thee for help and deliverance."

In reference to one of his daughters we find the
following concise entry :—"The 17th, came our friends
Henry Cleave and Jacob Phillips, and with them
Joshua Weymouth to visit my daughter, but she did
not like him ; so soon ended that courtship." Another
quaint entry is as follows :—"I got out to meeting
when the two young women, before spoken of, were
here, and were zealously concerned in meeting. . . . .
John Taylour stood up after them, and was forward in
it, which we often endeavoured but could not suppress."
In allusion to a Monthly Meeting he says, " Our business was managed with peace ; only Alice Bealing*
would put in a bit of cavilling, as is usual with dis-
content and forward folks, but it gave me liberty to
clear myself."

Early in 1715, in reference to the illness of his
daughter Anne, he writes :—

"I found our quietness was only maintained as we gave up
all our enjoyments into the Lord's hands ; yet when I should
consider her towardliness, her good understanding, and
elegancy of behaviour towards all, and in all cases (who was
now like to be taken away), it filled me frequently with
mourning and tears, so that my food seemed mingled with
weeping ; yet was the Lord's goodness near and upheld me,
as it did her also under pain scarcely tolerable, yet her spirit

---

* Apparently the wife of *E. B.*, to whom Thomas Gwin frequently alludes.

was free, and her resignation, as far as I could perceive, was fixed. . . . I was almost daily carried to her chamber. . . . She was kept in much patience and cheerfulness when her pain would suffer it."

About a month later we find recorded,—

"A day of great exercise ; the Lord taking from us our dearly beloved daughter Anne, who was a sweet creature in her living and dying, rarely accomplished, chaste, obedient, holy. She died in the twenty-third year of her age."

In allusion to a Monthly Meeting, Thomas Gwin writes of his concern "to press Friends to the leading of the Spirit as what would qualify for the service." He began with the text, "Days should speak, and multitude of years should teach wisdom. But there is a spirit in man : and the inspiration of the Almighty giveth them understanding."

It appears that on one Sabbath in every month a meeting was held at Come-to-good, in the parish of Kea, and was often very largely attended by the public. Thomas Gwin frequently went to this Monthly Meeting, as he calls it, and about this time he writes :—

"I rid to it with my daughter Pris. behind me. We found a great company, possibly near 1,000 people, and judging the house would not nearly contain them, we held our meeting in the yard. . . . I was forced to sit on horseback, and after John Taylour had exercised himself I began ; God in His infinite love does endeavour to reconcile man to Himself. He would have all men to be saved. . . . His covenant at Horeb, &c. The sending of the Son of His love to taste death for us."*

A month or two later the Cornish meetings were visited by Samuel Bownas and a Friend named Thomas Marsh, "in whose company," writes Thomas Gwin,

---

* A meeting is now held in this quaint old meeting-house (three miles distant from Truro Railway Station) four times a-year.

" we were plentifully refreshed, the former especially being a man excellently gifted. He spoke of the different gifts given to men for edifying, applying it home both to preachers and hearers, and of *the need there was for our labouring to know an increase in our gifts.* It was a seasonable instruction." At the parting meeting the next day they were "sweetly comforted together."

The next entry in the diary refers to a marriage " betwixt Christopher French and Edward Bealing's daughter." It seems that Samuel Bownas was present at the wedding entertainment, where Edward Bealing took great offence at his playful remark when "the syllabubs and toys" were placed on the table, that they were "like the maid's portion, much in show, little in substance!" Early in 1716 Thomas Gwin writes of receiving a letter from a Friend named Benjamin Coole, " signifying that his book about woman's preaching was under consideration of the Second-day's morning meeting, and there justified."

On the twenty-ninth anniversary of their wedding-day the wife of Thomas Gwin was not well enough to leave her chamber, and died after a very short illness. They had lived together, Thomas Gwin says,—

"with a growing affection all that time. We were many times afflicted together, especially in the loss of children: our common exercise greatly united us, till it pleased the Lord to dissolve the bond between us, and gather her to Himself. . . . Her works praise her. . . . Her illness kept me from meetings to attend on her; she being not willing to have me out of her sight, though I could not serve her by reason of my lameness as she did me, yet we conversed together much. . . . She was buried as nigh as could be to my daughter Anne."

A few months later, when one day feeling very low in a meeting, his heart was strengthened as he remembered the New Covenant which God would make with

His people, and he addressed those present on that
knowledge of Himself which God is ready to impart,
and pressed on all " a spiritual acquaintance therewith
that they might not lose so great a blessing through
heedlessness or stupidity." *   And now we arrive at
the last entry in the ponderous tome :—

" The Tenth Month [1716] I was greatly disabled with the
gout in my hands, with which I was hindered from writing.
. . . The Lord bear me up by His power, and the help of
His blessed spirit, that I may finish my course with joy, and
the testimony He hath given me to bear. Amen."

These words seem a fitting conclusion to the diary
of one who had laboured so patiently and unweariedly,
often in bodily weakness and suffering, for the advancement of Christ's kingdom on the earth.

In the summer of the following year Thomas Gwin
had an attack of palsy, which much impaired his
memory, but his life was prolonged until the 26th of
Tenth Month, 1720.   In his will he had remarked :—

" It is possible that had I sought after this world with
the earnestness that some of my contemporaries have done, I
might leave you a greater portion of it.   But . . . I hope it
will hold in the wearing, as not being got by fraud or
oppression, but by the blessing of God upon a moderate
industry."

Such is the simple summary of the quiet, uncvent-
ful life of one who gave good heed to the Apostolic
injunction, " *O, keep that which is committed to thy
trust.*"   God bids none of His children do more than
this ; neither does He authorise any of them to do
less.   Not in the spirit of bondage, but the love of
Christ constraining us, let us therefore ask, " Lord

---

* " The main reason why ' eye hath not seen ' is in our own
nature, and not because God has not prepared nor revealed such
things for our perception. To them that love Him, He reveals."—
J. R. H.

what wilt Thou have me to do ? " ; thankfully taking
the smallest service, or trustfully accepting the largest,
if it be indeed He who puts it into our hands.   Very
varied are the kinds of labour to be found in the
great field of the world ; but is not Thomas Gwin
right in saying, "This is a day wherein the Lord
calls every one of us into His vineyard to work " ?

> " God who at sundry times, in manners many,
>   Spake to the Fathers, and is speaking still ;
> Eager to find if ever or if any
>   Souls will obey and hearken to His will.
>
> .   .   .   .   .   .
>
> Whoso has felt the Spirit of the Highest,
>   Cannot confound nor doubt Him nor deny ;
> Yea, with one voice, O world, though thou deniest,
>   Stand thou on that side, for on this am I."

www.ingramcontent.com/pod-product-compliance
Lightning Source LLC
Chambersburg PA
CBHW020753020726
47495CB00008B/2414